Valley of
the Sun

BANTAM BOOKS BY LOUIS L'AMOUR
Ask your bookseller for the books you have missed.

NOVELS
Bendigo Shafter
Borden Chantry
Brionne
The Broken Gun
The Burning Hills
The Californios
Callaghen
Catlow
Chancy
The Cherokee Trail
Comstock Lode
Conagher
Crossfire Trail
Dark Canyon
Down the Long Hills
The Empty Land
Fair Blows the Wind
Fallon
The Ferguson Rifle
The First Fast Draw
Flint
Guns of the Timberlands
Hanging Woman Creek
The Haunted Mesa
Heller With a Gun
The High Graders
High Lonesome
Hondo
How the West Was Won
The Iron Marshal
The Key-Lock Man
Kid Rodelo
Kilkenny
Killoe
Kilrone
Kiowa Trail
Last of the Breed
Last Stand at Papago
  Wells
The Lonesome Gods
The Man Called Noon
The Man From
  Skibbereen
The Man From the
  Broken Hills
Matagorda

Milo Talon
The Mountain Valley War
North to the Rails
Over on the Dry Side
Passin' Through
The Proving Trail
The Quick and the Dead
Radigan
Reilly's Luck
The Rider of Lost Creek
Rivers West
The Shadow Riders
Shalako
Showdown at Yellow
  Butte
Silver Canyon
Sitka
Son of a Wanted Man
Taggart
The Tall Stranger
To Tame a Land
Tucker
Under the Sweetwater
  Rim
Utah Blaine
The Walking Drum
Westward the Tide
Where the Long Grass
  Blows

SHORT STORY COLLECTIONS
Bowdrie
Bowdrie's Law
Buckskin Run
Dutchman's Flat
The Hills of Homicide
Law of the Desert Born
Long Ride Home
Lonigan
Night Over the Solomons
The Outlaws of Mesquite
The Rider of the Ruby
  Hills
Riding for the Brand
The Strong Shall Live
The Trail to Crazy Man
Valley of the Sun

War Party
West From Singapore
Yondering

SACKETT TITLES
Sackett's Land
To the Far Blue
  Mountains
The Warrior's Path
Jubal Sackett
Ride the River
The Daybreakers
Sackett
Lando
Mojave Crossing
Mustang Man
The Lonely Men
Galloway
Treasure Mountain
Lonely on the Mountain
Ride the Dark Trail
The Sackett Brand
The Sky-Liners

THE HOPALONG
CASSIDY NOVELS
The Riders of the High
  Rock
The Rustlers of West Fork
The Trail to Seven Pines
Trouble Shooter

NONFICTION
Education of a
  Wandering Man
Frontier
The Sackett Companion:
  A Personal Guide to
  the Sackett Novels
A Trail of Memories:
  The Quotations of
  Louis L'Amour,
  compiled by Angelique
  L'Amour

POETRY
Smoke From This Altar

VALLEY OF
THE SUN

Frontier Stories by
LOUIS L'AMOUR

BANTAM BOOKS
NEW YORK TORONTO LONDON SYDNEY AUCKLAND

VALLEY OF THE SUN

A Bantam Book / May 1995

Library of Congress Cataloging-in-Publication Data

L'Amour, Louis, 1908–1988
    Valley of the sun : frontier stories / by Louis L'Amour.
        p.   cm.
    ISBN 0-553-09962-0
    1. Frontier and pioneer life—West (U.S.)—Fiction. 2. Western
stories. I. Title.
PS3523.A446V35   1995
813'.52—dc20   94-23224
                                                                   CIP

Published simultaneously in the United States and Canada

PRINTED IN THE UNITED STATES OF AMERICA

BVG   0   9   8   7   6   5   4   3   2   1

CONTENTS

We Shaped the Land with Our Guns / 1

West of the Pilot Range / 25

When a Texan Takes Over / 45

No Man's Mesa / 63

Gila Crossing / 77

Medicine Ground / 99

Valley of the Sun / 121

That Slash Seven Kid / 141

In Victorio's Country / 161

VALLEY OF
THE SUN

WE SHAPED THE LAND
WITH OUR GUNS

W e moved into the place on South Fork just before the snow went off. We had a hundred
head of cattle gathered from the canyons
along the Goodnight Trail, stray stuff from cattle outfits
moving north. Most of these cattle had been back in the
breaks for a couple of years and rounding them up was
man-killing labor, but we slapped our iron on them and
headed west.

Grass was showing green through the snow when we
got there and the cattle made themselves right at home.
Mountains to the east and north formed the base of a triangle of which the sides were shaped by creeks and the
apex by the junction of those creeks. It was a good four
miles from that apex to the spot we chose for our home
place, so we had all natural boundaries with good grass
and water. There were trees enough for fuel and shade.

The first two weeks we worked fourteen hours a day
building a cabin, cleaning out springs and throwing up a
stable, pole corrals, and a smokehouse. We had brought
supplies with us and we pieced them out with what game
we could shoot. By the time we had our building done,

our stock had decided they were home and were fattening up in fine shape.

We had been riding together for more than six months, which isn't long to know a man you go partners with. Tap Henry was a shade over thirty while I had just turned twenty-two when he hit the South Fork. We had met working for the Gadsen outfit, which took me on just west of Mobeetie while Tap joined up a ways further north. Both of us were a might touchy but we hit it off right from the start.

Tap Henry showed me the kind of man he was before we had been together three days. Some no-account riders had braced us to cut the herd, and their papers didn't look good to me nor to Tap. We were riding point when these fellers came up, and Tap didn't wait for the boss. He just told them it was tough, but they weren't cutting this herd. That led to words and one of these guys reached. Tap downed him and that was that.

He was a pusher, Tap was. When trouble showed up he didn't sidestep or wait for it. He walked right into the middle and kept crowding until the trouble either backed down or came through. Tall and straight standing, he was a fine, upright sort of man except for maybe a might of hardness around the eyes and mouth.

My home country was the Big Bend of Texas but most of my life had been lived south of the border. After I was sixteen the climate sort of agreed with me better. Tap drifted toward me one night when we were riding herd up in Wyoming.

"Rye," he said, that being a nickname for Ryan Tyler, "an hombre could go down in those breaks along the Goodnight Trail and sweep together a nice herd. Every outfit that ever come over this trail has lost stock, and lots of it is still back there."

"Uh-huh," I said, "and I know just the right spot for a ranch. Good grass, plenty of water and game." Then I told him about this place under the Pelado and he liked the sound of it. Whether he had any reason for liking an out-of-the-way place, I don't know. Me, I had plenty of reason, but I knew going back there might lead to trouble.

Two men can work together a long time without really knowing much about one another, and that was the way with me and Tap. We'd been in a couple of Comanche fights together and one with a Sioux war party. We worked together, both of us top hands and neither of us a shirker, and after a while we got a sort of mutual respect, although nobody could say we really liked each other.

Our first month was just ending when Jim Lucas showed up. We had been expecting him because we had seen a lot of Bar L cattle, and had run a couple of hundred head off our triangle of range when we first settled. He was not hunting us this day because his daughter was with him, and only one hand. Red, the puncher, had a lean face and a lantern jaw with cold gray eyes and two low, tied-down guns.

Lucas was a medium-built man who carried himself like he weighed a ton. He sat square and solid in the saddle, and you could see at a glance that he figured he was some shakes. Betty was eighteen that summer, slim but rounded, tan but lovely, with hair a golden web that tangled the sunlight. She had lips quick to laugh and the kind that looked easy to kiss. That morning she was wearing homespun jeans and a shirt like a boy, but no boy ever filled it out like she did.

Right off I spotted Red for a cold ticket to trouble. He stopped his horse off to one side, ready for disturbances.

"Howdy!" I straightened up from a dam I was building across a beginning wash. "Riding far?"

"That's my question." Lucas looked me over mighty cool. Maybe I looked like a sprout to him. While I'm nigh six feet tall I'm built slim and my curly hair makes me look younger than I am. "My outfit's the Bar L, and this is my graze."

Tap Henry had turned away from the corral and

walked down toward us. His eyes went from Lucas to the redhead and back. Me, I was off to one side. Tap wore his gun tied down but I carried mine shoved into my waistband.

"We're not riding," Tap replied, "we're staying. We're claiming all the range from the creeks to the Pelado."

"Sorry, boys"—Lucas was still friendly although his voice had taken on a chill, "that's all my range and I wasn't planning on giving any of it up. Besides"—he never took his eyes off Tap Henry—"I notice a lot of vented brands on your cattle. All I saw, in fact."

"See any of yours?" Tap was quiet. Knowing how touchy he could be, I was worried and surprised at the same time. This was one fight he wasn't pushing and I was sure glad of it.

"No, I didn't," Lucas admitted, "but that's neither here nor there. We don't like outfits that stock vented brands."

"Meaning anything in particular?" Tap asked.

Quiet as he was, there was a veiled threat in his tone now and Jim Lucas seemed suddenly to realize that his daughter sat beside him. Also, for the first time he seemed to understand that he was dealing with a different kind of man than he had believed.

"Meaning only," he said carefully, "that we don't like careless brands on this range or small outfits that start that way."

Tap was reasonable. More so than I had expected. "We rounded those cattle up," he explained, "from the canyons along the Goodnight. They are abandoned trail herd stock, and we got letters from three of the biggest outfits giving us title to all of their stuff we can find. Most of the other brands are closed out or in Montana. We aim to run this stock and its increase."

"Maybe. But run it somewheres else. This is my range. Get off it."

"Maybe you take in too much territory?" Tap suggested. "My partner and I aren't hunting trouble, but I don't reckon you hold any deed to this land from the government, the people, or God. You just laid claim to it. We figure you got your hands full, and we lay claim to the triangle of range described."

"Boss," Red interrupted, "I've seen this hombre somewhere before."

Tap did not change expression but it seemed to me that his face went a shade whiter under the tan. Betty was looking worried and several times she had started as if to interrupt.

"We can be neighbors," Tap persisted. "We wanted our own outfit. Now we've got it and we intend to keep it."

Lucas was about to make a hot reply when Betty interrupted. She had been looking at me. Everybody else seemed to have forgotten me and that pleased me just as well. My old gray hat was ragged on the crown and my hair hung down to my shirt collar. My buckskin pullover shirt was unlaced at the neck, my jeans were patched, and my boots were weather-worn and scarred by horns.

Betty said quietly, "Why don't you and your friend come to the dance at Ventana Saturday night? We would all enjoy having you."

Jim Lucas scowled and started impatiently as if to speak, but then he seemed to see me for the first time. His mouth opened, but he swallowed whatever it was he was going to say. What held him I do not know but he stared hard at me.

"Sure," I replied to Betty, "we would be glad to come. We want to be neighborly like my partner said. You can expect us."

Lucas wheeled his horse. "We'll talk about this again. You've been warned." He looked at Tap when he said it, and then started off with Betty beside him.

Red lingered, staring at Tap. "Where was it," he said, "that we met before?"

"We never met." Tap's voice was flat and hard. "And let's hope you don't remember."

That was more of a warning than I ever heard Tap give anybody. Usually, if you asked for it he just hauled iron and then planted you.

We started for the cabin together and Tap glanced around at me.

"Ever sling a six-gun, Rye? If war comes we'll have to scrap to hold our land."

"If it comes"—I pulled off my shirt to wash—"don't you worry. I'll hold up my end."

"That gal . . ." he commented suddenly, "really something, wasn't she?"

Now, why should that have made me sore?

Saturday morning we shaved early and dressed for the dance. It was a long ride ahead of us and we wanted to get started. When I got my stuff out of my warbag I looked down at those worn and scuffed gun belts and the two six-shooters. Just for a minute there, I hesitated, then I stuffed a pair of old jeans in atop them.

Then I slicked up. My hair was long, all right, but my black broadcloth suit was almost new and tailored to fit. My clothes have to be tailored because my shoulders are so broad and my waist so slim I can never buy me a hand-me-down. With it I wore a gray wool shirt and a black neckerchief, and topped it off with my best hat, which was black and flat-crowned.

Tap was duded up some, too. When he looked at me I could see the surprise in his eyes, and he grinned. "You're a handsome lad, Rye! A right handsome lad!" But when he'd said it his face chilled as if he had thought of something unpleasant. He added only one thing. "You wearing a gun? You better."

My hand slapped my waistband and flipped back my coat. The butt of my Russian .44 was there, ready to hand.

That draw from the waistband is one of the fastest. There was no reason why I should tell him about the other gun in the shoulder holster. That was a newfangled outfit that some said had been designed by Ben Thompson, and if it was good enough for Ben, it was good enough for me.

It was a twenty-five-mile ride but we made good time. At the livery stable I ordered a bait of corn for the horses. Tap glanced at me.

"Costs money," he said tersely.

"Uh-huh, but a horse can run and stay with it on corn. We ain't in no position to ride slow horses."

Betty was wearing a blue gown the color of her eyes, and while there were a half dozen right pretty girls there, none of them could stand with her. The nearest was a dark-eyed señorita who was all flash and fire. She glanced at me once from those big dark eyes, then paused for another look.

Tap wasted no time. He had crossed the room to Betty and was talking to her. Her eyes met mine across the room, but Tap was there first and I wasn't going to crowd him. The Mex girl was lingering, so I asked for the dance and got it. Light as a feather she was, and slick and easy on her feet. We danced that one and another, and then an Irish girl with freckles on her nose showed up, and after her I danced again with Margita Lopez. Several times I brushed past Betty and we exchanged glances. Hers were very cool.

The evening was almost over when suddenly we found ourselves side by side. "Forgotten me?" There was a thin edge on her voice. "If you remember, I invited you."

"You also invited my partner, and you seemed mighty busy, so I—"

"I saw you," she retorted. "Dancing with Margita."

"She's a good dancer, and mighty pretty."

"Oh? You think so?" Her chin came up and battle flashed in her eyes. "Maybe you think—!" The music

7

started right then so I grabbed her and moved into the dance and she had no chance to finish whatever she planned to say.

There are girls and girls. About Betty there was something that hit me hard. Somehow we wound up out on the porch of this old ranch house turned school, and we started looking for stars. Not that we needed any.

"I hope you stay," she said suddenly.

"Your father doesn't," I replied, "but we will."

She was worried. "Father's set in his ways, Rye, but it isn't only he. The one you may have trouble with is Chet Bayless. He and Jerito."

"Who?" Even as I asked the question the answer was in my mind.

"Jerito Juarez. He's a gunman who works for Bayless. A very fine vaquero, but he's utterly vicious and a killer. As far as that goes, Bayless is just as bad. Red Corram, who works for Dad, runs with them some."

Jerito Juarez was a name I was not likely to forget, and inside me something turned cold. Just then the door opened and Tap Henry came out. When he saw us standing close together on the dark porch his face, in the light of the door, was not pleasant to see.

"I was hunting you, Betty. Our dance is most over."

"Oh! I'm sorry! I didn't realize . . . !"

Tap looked over her head at me. "We've trouble coming," he said, "watch your step."

Walking to the end of the porch, I stepped down and started toward the horses. Under the trees and in the deep shadows I heard voices.

"Right now," a man was saying, "ride over there and go through their gear. I want to know who they are. Be mighty careful, because if that Tap is who I think he is, he'll shoot mighty fast and straight."

Another voice muttered and then there was a chink

of coins. In an open place under the trees I could vaguely distinguish three men.

The first voice added, "An' when you leave, set fire to the place."

That was the man I wanted, but they separated and I knew if I followed the two that went back toward the dance, then the man who was to burn us out would get away. Swiftly, I turned after the latter, and when he reached his horse he was in the lights from the dance. The man was a half-breed, a suspected rustler known as Kiowa Johnny.

Stepping into the open, I said to him, "You ain't going noplace to burn anybody out. If you want to live, unbuckle those gun belts and let 'em fall. And be mighty careful!"

Kiowa stood there, trying to make me out. The outline of me was plain to him, but my face must have been in shadow. He could see both hands at my sides and they held no gun, nor was there a gun in sight. Maybe he figured it was a good gamble that I was unarmed. He grabbed for his gun.

My .44 Russian spoke once, a sharp, emphatic remark, and then acrid power smoke drifted and above the sound of the music within I heard excited voices. Kiowa Johnny lay sprawled on the hard-packed earth.

Wanting no gunfights or questions, I ducked around the corner of the dance hall and back to the porch where I had been standing with Betty. The door that opened to the porch was blocked by people, but all were looking toward the dance floor. One of them was Margita. Moving among them, I touched her arm and we moved out on the floor together.

Right away she knew something was wrong. She was quick, that girl. And then the music stopped and Jim Lucas was standing in the middle of the floor with Sheriff Fred Tetley.

"Kiowa Johnny's been killed," Tetley said. "Looks like he had a fair shake. Who done it?"

9

Tap was right in the middle of things with Betty and I saw Red frown as his eyes located him. Almost automatically, those eyes searched me out. He was puzzled when he looked away.

"Had it comin' for years!" A gray-haired man near me was speaking. "Maybe we won't lose so many cows now."

"Who killed him?" Tetley demanded irritably. "Speak up, whoever it was. It's just a formality."

My reasons for not speaking were the best ones, so I waited. Lucas put a hand on the sheriff's shoulder.

"Best forget it, Fred. His gun was half-drawn, so he made a try for it. Whoever shot him was fast and could really shoot. That bullet was dead center through the heart despite the bad light!"

His eyes went to Tap Henry, and then momentarily, they rested on me. Margita had me by the arm and I felt her fingers tighten. When she looked up at me she said quietly, "You saw it?"

Somehow, something about her was warm, understanding. "I did it." My voice was low and we were a little apart from the others. "There are good reasons why nobody must know now. It was quite fair." Simply, then, but without mentioning Red, I told her what I had heard.

She accepted my story without question. All of them at the dance knew every effort would be made to run us off South Fork, so my story was no surprise. Some women could keep a secret and I was sure she was one of them.

That we were on very shaky ground here both Tap and I knew. It was not only Lucas. As the biggest of the ranchers, and the one whose actual range had been usurped, he had the most right to complain, but Bayless of the Slash B was doing the most talking, and from what I had heard, he had a way of taking the law into his own hands.

Tap joined me. "You see that shooting?" he asked. Then without awaiting a reply, he continued, "Guess he had it coming, but I wonder who did it? That's the kind of shooting Wes Hardin does or the Laredo Kid. Heard anything?"

"Only that Johnny had it coming. He was the kind who might be hired to dry-gulch a man or burn him out."

Tap glanced at me quickly, but before he could speak, Betty hurried up to us.

"You two had better go," she whispered. "There's some talk around and some of the men are hunting trouble."

She spoke to both of us, but she looked at me. Tap shifted his feet. "What do you expect us to do?" he demanded. "Run?"

"Of course not!" she protested. "But why not avoid trouble until I can talk some sense into Dad?"

"That's reasonable, Tap. Let's go."

"If you want to back down"—his voice was irritable and he spoke more sharply than he ever had to me—"go ahead and go! I say face 'em and show 'em they've got a fight on their hands!"

The contempt in his voice got to me but I took a couple of deep breaths before I answered him. "Don't talk like that, Tap. When a fight comes, I'll be ready for it, only why not give Betty a chance? Once the shooting starts there'll be no more chance."

Two men shoved through the door followed by a half dozen others. My pulse jumped and I grabbed Tap's arm. "Let's get out of here! There's Chet Bayless and Jerito Juarez!"

How could I miss that lithe, wiry figure? Betty Lucas gave me a swift, measuring look of surprise. Tap shook my hand from his arm and shot me a glance like he'd give to a yellow dog. "All right," he said, "let's go! I can't face them alone!"

What they must be thinking of me I could guess, but all I could think of was facing Bayless and Jerito in that crowded room. And I knew Jerito and what would happen when he saw me. The crowd would make no difference, nor the fact that innocent people might be killed.

Betty avoided my eyes and moved away from my hand when I turned to say good-bye, so I merely followed Tap Henry out the door. All the way home he never said a word, nor the next morning until almost noon.

"You stay away from Betty," he said then, "she's my girl."

"Betty's wearing no brand that I can see," I told him quietly, "and until somebody slaps an iron on her, I'm declaring myself in the running.

"I don't," I continued, "want trouble between us. We've rode a lot of rivers together, and we've got trouble started here. We can hold this place and build a nice spread."

"What about last night?" His voice was cold. "You took water."

"Did you want to start throwing lead in a room full of kids and women? Besides, fightin' ain't enough. Anybody with guts and a gun can fight. It's winning that pays off."

His eyes were measuring me. "What does that mean?" That I'd fallen in his estimation, I knew. Maybe I'd never stood very high.

"That we choose the time to fight," I said. "Together we can whip them, but just showing how tough we are won't help. We've got to get the odds against us as low as we can."

"Maybe you're right." He was reluctant to agree. "I seen a man lynched once because he shot a kid accidental in a gunfight." He sized me up carefully. "You seemed scared of those three."

We looked at each other over the coffee cups and inside I felt a slow hot resentment rising, but I kept it down. "I'm not," I told him, "only Chet Bayless is known for eight square killings. Down Sonora way Jerito is figured to have killed twice that many. That Jerito is poison mean, and we can figure on getting hurt even if we win."

"Never figured them as tough as all that," Tap muttered. Then he shot me a straight, hard glance. "How come you know so much about 'em?"

"Bayless," I said carefully, "is a Missourian. Used to run with the James boys, but settled in Eagle Pass. Jerito—everybody in Sonora knows about him."

The next few days followed pleasant and easy, and we worked hard without any words between us beyond those necessary to work and live. It irritated me that Tap doubted me.

On the fourth afternoon I was stripping the saddle off my steeldust when I heard them coming. A man who lives like I do has good ears and eyes or he don't live at all. "Tap!" I called to him low but sharp. "Riders coming!"

He straightened up, then shot a look at me. "Sure?"

"Yeah." I threw my saddle over a log we used for that and slicked my rifle out of the scabbard and leaned it by the shed door. "Just let 'em come."

They rode into the yard in a compact bunch and Tap Henry walked out to meet them. Bayless was there, riding with Jim Lucas, but Jerito was not. The minute I saw that I felt better. When they first showed I had stepped back into the shed out of sight. There were a dozen of them in the bunch and they drew up. Bayless took the play before Lucas could get his mouth open.

"Henry!" He said it hard and short. "You been warned. Get your stuff. We're burning you out!"

Tap waited while you could count three before he spoke. "Like hell," he said.

"We want no nesters around here! Once one starts they all come! And we want nobody with your record!"

"My record?" Tap had guts, I'll give him that. He stepped once toward Bayless. "Who says I—!"

"I do!" It was Red Corram. "You rode with that Roost outfit in the Panhandle."

"Sure did." Tap smiled. "I reckon not a man here but ain't misbranded a few head. I ain't doing it now."

"That's no matter!" Bayless was hard. "Get out or be buried here!"

Lucas cleared his throat and started to speak.

Tap looked at him. "You feel that way, Lucas?"

"I'm not for killing," he said, "but—!"

"I am!" Bayless was tough about it. "I say they get out or shoot it out!"

Tap Henry had taken one quick glance toward the shed when they rode up, and when he saw me gone he never looked again. I knew he figured he was all alone. Well, he wasn't. Not by a long shot. Now it was my turn.

Stepping out into the open, I said, "That go for me, too, Chet?"

He turned sharp around at the voice and stared at me. My hat was pulled low and the only gun I wore was that .44 Russian in my waistband. I took another step out and a little bit toward the trail, which put Bayless in a bad spot. If he turned to face me his side was to Tap. "Who are you?" Bayless demanded. He was a big blue-jowled man, but right now the face under those whiskers looked pale.

"The name is Tyler, Chet. Ryan Tyler. Don't reckon you ever heard *that* name before, did you now?" Without turning my head, I said to Tap, but loud enough so they could all hear me. "Tap, if they want to open this ball, I want Bayless."

They were flabbergasted, you could see it. Here I was, an unknown kid, stepping out to call a rancher known as a gunman. It had them stopped, and nobody quite knew what to say.

"Lucas," I said, "you ain't a fool. You got a daughter and a nice ranch. You got some good boys. If this shooting starts we can't miss Bayless or you."

It was hot, that afternoon, with the clouds fixing up to rain. Most of the snow was gone now, and there was the smell of spring in the air.

"Me, I ain't riding nowhere until I've a mind to. I'm

fixing to stay right here, and if it's killing you want, then you got a chance to start it. But for every one of us you bury, you'll bury three of you."

Tap Henry was as surprised as they were, I could see that, and it was surprise that had them stopped, not anything else. That surprise wasn't going to last, I knew. Walking right up to them, I stopped again, letting my eyes sweep over them, then returning to Bayless.

"Why don't you get down, Chet? If you go for that gun you better have solid footing. You don't want to miss that first shot, Chet. If you miss it you'll never get another.

"You aimed to do some burning, Chet. Why don't you get down and start your fire? Start it with a gun like your coyote friend did?" Without shifting his eyes, Bayless stared, and then slowly he kicked one foot out of a stirrup. "That's right, Chet. Get down. I want you on the ground, where you don't have so far to fall. This hombre" —I said it slow—"paid Kiowa Johnny to burn us out. I heard 'em. I gave Johnny a chance to drop his guns and would have made him talk, but he wanted to take a chance. He took it."

"You killed Johnny?" Lucas demanded, staring at me. "He was supposed to be a fast man with a gun."

"Him?" The contempt was thick in my voice. "Not even middling fast." My eyes had never left Bayless. "You want to start burning, Chet, you better get down."

Chet Bayless was bothered. It had been nigh two years since he had seen me and I'd grown over an inch in height and some in breadth of shoulder since then. My face was part shaded by that hat and he could just see my mouth and chin. But he didn't like it. There was enough of me there to jar his memory and Chet Bayless, while fast with a gun, was no gambler. With Jerito or Red there, he would have gambled, but he knew Red was out of it because of Tap.

"Lucas," I said, "you could be riding in better company. Bayless ain't getting off that horse. He's got no

15

mind to. He figures to live awhile longer. You fellers better figure it this way. Tap and me, we like this place. We aim to keep it. We also figure to run our own cows, but to be fair about it, anytime you want to come over here and cut a herd of ours, come ahead. That goes for you—not for Bayless or any of his gun-handy outfit."

Chet Bayless was sweating. Very careful, he had put his toe back in the stirrup. Jim Lucas shot one glance at him, and then his old jaw set.

"Let's go!" He wheeled his horse and without another word they rode away.

Only Red looked back. He looked at Tap, not me. "See you in town!" he said.

Henry called after him. "Anytime, Red! Just anytime at all!"

When the last of them had gone he turned and looked at me. "That was a tough play, kid. S'pose Bayless had drawed on you?"

"Reckon he'd of died," I said simply enough, "but I didn't figure he would. Chet's a cinch player. Not that he ain't good with that Colt. He is—plenty!"

Walking back, I got my rifle. "Gosh amighty, I'm sure hungry!" I said, and that was all. What Tap thought of it, I had no idea. Only a couple of times I caught him sizing me up. And then the following night he rode off and I knew where he was riding. He was gone a-courting of Betty Lucas.

That made me sore but there was nothing I could do about it. He sort of hinted that Margita was my dish, but that wasn't so. She was all wrapped up in some vaquero who worked for her old man, although not backward about a little flirtation.

One thing I knew. Chet Bayless was going to talk to Jerito and then they were going to come for me. Jerito Juarez had good reason to hate me, and he would know me for the Laredo Kid.

Me, I'd never figured nor wanted the name of a gunfighter, but it was sort of natural-like for me to use a gun easy and fast. At sixteen a kid can be mighty touchy about not being growed up. I was doing a man's job on the NOB outfit when Ed Keener rawhided me into swinging on him. He went down, and when he came up he hauled iron. Next thing I knew Keener was on the ground drilled dead center and I had a smoking gun in my hand with all the hands staring at me like a calf had suddenly growed into a mountain lion right before them.

Keener had three brothers, so I took out and two of them cornered me in Laredo. One of them never got away from that corner, and the other lived after three months in bed. Meanwhile, I drifted into Mexico and worked cows down there. In El Paso I shot it out with Jerito's brother and downed him, and by that time they were talking me up as another Billy the Kid. They called me Laredo for the town I hailed from, but when I went back thataway I went into the Nueces country, where the third Keener braced me and fitted himself into the slot of Boot Hill alongside his brothers.

After that I'd gone kind of hog-wild, only not killing anybody but some ornery Comanches. Howsoever, I did back down a sheriff at Fort Griffin, shot a gun out of another's hand in Mobeetie, and backed down three tough hands at Doan's Crossing. By that time everybody was talking about me, so I drifted where folks didn't know Ryan Tyler was the Laredo gunfighter.

Only Chet Bayless knew because Chet had been around when I downed the Keeners. And Jerito knew.

After that I quit wearing guns in sight and avoided trouble all I could. That was one reason this out-of-the-way ranch under the Pelado appealed to me, and why I avoided trouble all I could.

It must have been midnight and I'd been asleep a couple of hours when a horse came hell a-whoppin' down the trail and I heard a voice holler the house. Unloading from my bunk, I grabbed my rifle and gave a call from the door. Then I got a shock, for it was Betty Lucas.

"Rye! Come quick! Tap killed Lon Beatty and a mob's got him! They'll hang him!"

No man ever got inside of his clothes faster than me, but this time I dumped my warbag and grabbed those belted guns. Swinging the belts around me, I stuck my .44 Russian into my waistband for good measure and ran for my horse. Betty had him caught and a saddle on him, so all I had to do was cinch up and climb aboard.

"They are at Cebolla!" she called to me. "Hurry!"

Believe me, I lit a shuck. That steeldust I was on was a runner and chock-full of corn. He stretched his legs and ran like a singed cat, so it wasn't long until the lights of Cebolla showed. Then I was slowing down with a dark blob in the road ahead of me with some torches around it. They had Tap, all right, had him backward on his horse with a rope around his neck. He looked mighty gray around the gills but was cussing them up one side and down the other. Then I came up, walking my horse.

"All right, boys!" I let it out loud. "Fun's over! No hanging tonight!"

"Who says so?" They were all peering my way, so I gave it to them.

"Why, this here's Rye Tyler," I said, "but down So-nora way they call me Laredo, or the Laredo Kid. I've got a Winchester here and three loaded pistols, and I ain't the kind to die quick, so if some of you hombres figure you'd like to make widows and orphans of your wives and kids, just start reaching.

"I ain't," I said, "a mite particular about who I shoot. I ain't honing to kill anybody, but knowing Tap, I figure if he shot anybody it was a fair shooting. Now back off, and back off easylike. My hands both work fast, so I can use both guns at once. That figures twelve shots if you stop me then, but I got a Winchester and another gun. Me, I ain't missed a shot since I was eleven years old, so anybody fixin' to die sure don't need to go to no trouble tonight!"

Nobody moved, but out of the tail of my eye I could see some change of expression on Tap's face.

"He reached first," Tap said.

"But he was just a kid!" Who that was, I don't know. It sounded like Gravel Brown, who bummed drinks around Ventana.

"His gun was as big as a man's," Tap said, "and he's seventeen, which makes him old as I was when I was segundo for a fighting outfit driving to Ogallala."

Brown was no fighter. "Gravel," I said, "you move up easylike and take that noose off Tap's neck, and if you so much as nudge him or that horse they'll be pattin' over your face with a spade come daybreak."

Gravel Brown took that noose off mighty gentle. I'd walked my horse up a few steps while Gravel untied Tap's hands, and then restored his guns.

"You may get away with this now, Tyler," somebody said, "but you and Tap better take your luck and make tracks. You're through here. We want no gunslingers in this country."

"No?" That made me chuckle. "All right, amigo, you tell that to Chet Bayless, Red Corram, and most of all, Jerito Juarez. If they go, we will. Until then, our address is the Pelado, and if you come a-visiting, the coffee's always on. If you come hunting trouble, why I reckon we can stir you up a mess of that." I backed my horse a couple of feet. "Come on, Tap. These boys need their sleep. Let 'em go home."

We sat there side by each and watched them go. They didn't like it, but none of them wanted to be a dead hero. When they had gone, Tap turned to me.

"Saved my bacon, kid." He started riding, and after a ways he turned to me. "That straight about you being the Laredo gunfighter?"

"Uh-huh. No reason to broadcast it."

"And I was wondering if you'd fight! How foolish can a man be?"

It set like that for a week, and nobody showed up around South Fork and nobody bothered us. Tap, he went away at night occasional, but he never said anything and I didn't ask any questions. Me, I stayed away. This was Tap's play, and I figured if she wanted Tap she did not want me. Her riding all that way sure looked like she did want him, though. Then came Saturday and I saddled up and took a packhorse. Tap studied me, and said finally, "I reckon I better side you."

"Don't reckon you better, Tap," I said, "things been too quiet. I figure they think we'll do just that, come to town together and leave this place empty. When we got back we'd either be burned out or find them sitting in the cabin with Winchesters. You hold it down here."

Tap got up. His face was sharp and hard as ever, but he looked worried. "But they might gang you, kid. No man can buck a stacked deck."

"Leave it to me," I said, "and we've got no choice anyway. We need grub."

Ventana was dozing in the sun when I walked the steeldust down the main alley of the town. A couple of sleepy old codgers dozed against the sun-backed front of a building, a few horses stood three-legged at the tie rail. Down the street a girl sat in a buckboard, all stiff and starched in a gingham gown, seeing city life and getting broken into it.

Nobody was in the store but the owner himself and he was right pert getting my stuff ready. As before, I was wearing three guns in sight and a fourth in that shoulder holster under my jacket. If they wanted war they could have it.

When my stuff was ready I stashed it near the back door and started out the front. The storekeeper looked at me, then said, "You want to live you better hightail it. They been waiting for you."

I shoved my hat back on my head and grinned at him. "Thanks, mister, but that sure wouldn't be neighborly of me, would it? Folks wait for me shouldn't miss their appointment. I reckon I'll go see what they have to say."

"They'll say it with lead." He glowered at me, but I could see he was friendly.

"Then I guess I can speak their language," I said. "Was a time I was a pretty fluent conversationalist in that language. Maybe I still am."

"They'll be in the Ventana Saloon," he said, "and a couple across the street. There'll be at least four."

When I stepped out on the boardwalk about twenty hombres stepped off it. I mean that street got as empty as a panhandler's pocket, so I started for the Ventana, watching mighty careful and keeping close to the buildings along the right-hand side of the street. That store across the street where two of them might be was easy to watch.

An hombre showed in the window of the store and I waited. Then Chet Bayless stepped out of the saloon. Red Corram came from the store. And Jerito Juarez suddenly walked into the center of the street. Another hombre stood in an alleyway and they had me fairly boxed. "Come in at last, huh?" Bayless chuckled. "Now we see who's nestin' on this range!"

"Hello, Jerito," I called, "nobody hung you yet? I been expecting it."

"Not unteel I keel you!" Jerito stopped and spread his slim legs wide.

Mister, I never seen anything look as mean and ornery as that hombre did then! He had a thin face with long narrow black eyes and high cheekbones. It wasn't the rest of that outfit I was watching, it was him. That boy was double-eyed dynamite, all charged with hate for me and my kind.

"You never seen the day," I said, "when you could

tear down my meathouse, Jerito." Right then I felt cocky. There was a devil in me, all right, a devil I was plumb scared of. That was why I ducked and kept out of sight, because when trouble came to me I could feel that old lust to kill getting up in my throat and no smart man wants to give rein to that sort of thing. Me, I rode herd on it, mostly, but right now it was in me and it was surging high. Right then if somebody had told me for certain sure that I was due to die in that street, I couldn't have left it.

My pulse was pounding and my breath coming short and I stood there shaking and all filled with wicked eagerness, just longing for them to open the ball.

And then Betty Lucas stepped into the street.

She must have timed it. She must have figured she could stop that killing right there. She didn't know Chet Bayless, Corram, and those others. They would fire on a woman. And most Mexicans wouldn't, but she didn't know Jerito Juarez. He would have shot through his mother to kill me, I do believe.

Easylike, and gay, she walked out there in that dusty street, swinging a sunbonnet on her arm, just as easy as you'd ever see. Somebody yelled at her and somebody swore, but she kept coming, right up to me.

"Let's go, Rye," she said gently. "You'll be killed. Come with me."

Lord knows, I wanted to look at her, but my eyes never wavered. "Get out of the street, Betty. I made my play. I got to back it up. You go along now."

"They won't shoot if you're with me," she said, "and you must come, *now!*" There was awful anxiety in her eyes, and I knew what it must have taken for her to come out into that street after me. And my eyes must have flickered because I saw Jerito's hand flash.

Me? I never moved so fast in my life! I tripped up Betty and sprawled her in the dust at my feet and almost as she hit dust my right-hand gun was making war talk across her body, lying there so slim and lovely, angry and scared.

Jerito's gun and mine blasted fire at the same second, me losing time with getting Betty down. Something ripped at my sleeve and then I stepped over her and had both guns going, and from somewhere another gun started and Jerito was standing there with blood running down his face and it all twisted with a kind of wild horror above the flame-stabbing .44 that pounded death at me.

Bayless I took out with my left-hand gun, turning him with a bullet through his right elbow, a bullet that was making a different man of him, although I didn't know it then.

He never again was able to flash a fast gun!

Jerito suddenly broke and lunged toward me. He was blood all over the side of his head and face and shoulder, but he was still alive and in a killing mood. He came closer and we both let go at point-blank range, but I was maybe a split second faster and that bullet hit bone.

When a bullet hits bone a man goes down, and he went down and hard. He rolled over and stared up at me.

"You *fast*! You . . . *diablo*!" His face twisted and he died right there, and when I looked up, Tap Henry was standing alongside the Ventana Saloon with a smoking gun in his hand, and that was a Christian town.

That's what I mean. We made believers out of them that day in the dusty street on a warm, still afternoon. Tap and me, we made them see what it meant to tackle us and the town followed the ranchers and they followed Jim Lucas when he came down to shake hands and call it a truce.

Betty was alongside me, her face dusty, but not so pale anymore, and Tap walked over, holstering his gun. He held out his hand, and I shook it. We'd been riding partners for months, but from that day on we were *friends*.

"You and me, kid," he said, "we can whip the world! Or we can make it plumb peaceful! I reckon our troubles are over."

"No hard feelings?" One of my arms was around Betty.

23

"Not one!" He grinned at me. "You was always head man with her. And us? Well, I never knowed a man I'd rather ride the river with!"

There's more cattle on the Pelado now, and the great bald dome of the mountain stands above the long green fields where the cattle graze, and where the horses' coats grow shining and beautiful, and there are two houses there now, and Tap has one of them with a girl from El Paso, and I have the other with Betty.

We came when the country was young and wild, and it took men to curry the roughness out of it, and we knew the smell of gunsmoke, the buffalo-chip fires, and the long swell of the prairie out there where the cattle rolled north to feed a nation on short-grass beef.

We helped to shape that land, hard and beautiful as it was, and the sons we reared, Tap and me, they ride where we rode, and when the day comes, they can carry their guns, too, to fight for what we fought for, the long, beautiful smell of the wind with the grass under it, and the purple skies with the slow smoke of home fires burning.

All that took a lot of building, took blood, lead, death and cattle, but we built it, and there she stands, boys. How does she look now?

WEST OF THE
PILOT RANGE

W ard McQueen let the strawberry roan amble placidly down the hillside toward the spring in the cottonwoods. He pulled his battered gray sombrero lower over his eyes and squinted at the meadow.

There were close to three hundred head of white-faced cattle grazing there and a rider on a gray horse was staring up toward him. The man carried a rifle across his saddle, and as McQueen continued to head down the hillside, the rider turned his horse and started quickly forward.

He was a powerfully built man with a thick neck and a shock of untrimmed red hair. His hard, little, blue eyes stared at McQueen.

"Who are yuh?" the redhead demanded. "Where yuh goin'?"

McQueen brought the roan to a stop. The redhead's voice angered him and he was about to make a sharp reply when he noticed a movement in the willows along the stream and caught the gleam of a rifle. "I'm just ridin' through," he replied quietly. "Why?"

"Which way yuh come from?" The redhead was suspicious. "Lots of rustlers around here."

McQueen chuckled. "Well, I ain't one," he said cheerfully. "I been ridin' down Arizona way. Thought I'd change my luck by comin' north."

"Saddle tramp, eh?" Red grinned a little himself, revealing broken yellow teeth. "Huntin' a job?"

"Might be." McQueen looked at the cattle. "Yore spread around here?"

"No. We're drivin' 'em west. The boss bought 'em down Wyomin' way. We could use a hand. Forty a month and grub, bonus when we git there."

"Sounds good," McQueen admitted. "How far yuh drivin'?"

" 'Bout a hundred miles further." Red hesitated a little. "Come talk to the boss. We got a couple of riders, but we'll need another, all right."

They started down the hill toward the cottonwoods and willows. Ward McQueen glanced thoughtfully at the cattle. They were in good shape. It was unusual to see cattle in such good shape after so long a drive. And the last seventy-five miles of it across one of the worst deserts in the west. Of course, they might have been here several days, and green grass, rest, and water helped a lot.

A tall man in black stepped from the willows as they approached. There was no sign of a rifle, yet Ward was certain it was the same man. Rustlers or Indians would have a hard time closing in on this bunch, he thought.

"Boss," Red said, "this here's a saddle tramp from down Arizony way. Huntin' him a job. I figgered he might be a good hand to have along. This next forty miles or so is Injun country."

The man stared at McQueen through close-set, black eyes, and one hand lifted to the carefully trimmed mustache.

"My name is Hoyt," he said sharply. "Iver Hoyt. I do need another hand. Where yuh from?"

"Texas," McQueen drawled. "Been ridin' in south of Sante Fe and over Arizona way." He took out the makin's and started to build a cigarette.

Hoyt was a sharp-looking man with a hard, ratlike face. He wore a gun under his Prince Albert coat.

"All right, Red, put him to work." Hoyt looked up at Red. "Work him on the same basis as the others, understand?"

"Sure," Red said, grinning. "Oh, sure. The same way."

Hoyt turned and strode away through the trees toward a faint column of smoke that arose from beyond the willows.

Red turned. "My name's Red Naify," he said. "What do I call you?"

"I'm Ward McQueen. They call me Ward. How's it for grub?"

"Sure thing." Red turned his horse through the willows. McQueen followed, frowning thoughtfully.

Something about the setup didn't please him. It was another of those hunches of his. He always tried to disregard them, but somehow it just wouldn't work.

There was no danger about the cattle drifting. They had just crossed a desert, if Red's story was true, and there was no grass within miles as green and lush as this in the meadow. And water was scarce. So why had Naify been out there with the cattle close to grub call? And why had Iver Hoyt been down in the trees with a rifle?

It was on the edge of Indian country, he knew. There had been rumors of raids by a band of Piute warriors from the Thousand Spring Valley, north of here. He shrugged. What the devil? He was probably being unduly suspicious about the outfit.

Two riders were sitting over the fire and they looked up when he approached. One was a squat man with a bald head. The other a slim, pleasant-looking youngster who looked up, grinning, when they rode near.

"This is 'Baldy' Jackson," Naify said. "He's cook and nightrider usually. The kid is Bud Fox. Baldy an' Bud, this is Ward McQueen."

Baldy's head came up with a jerk and he almost dropped the frying pan. Naify looked at him in surprise and so did Bud. Baldy looked around slowly, his eyes slanting at Ward, without expression.

"Howdy," he said, and turned back to his cooking.

Bud Fox brought up an armful of wood and began poking sticks into the fire. He glanced at Baldy curiously, but the cook did not look up again.

When they had finished eating, Hoyt saddled a fresh horse and mounted up. Red Naify got up and sauntered slowly over to the edge of camp, out of hearing distance. The two talked seriously while Bud Fox lay with his head on his saddle, dozing. Baldy picked idly at his teeth, staring into the fire. One or twice the older man looked up, glancing toward the two standing at the edge of the willows.

He picked up a heavier stick and placed it on the fire.

"You from Lincoln?" he asked, low-voiced. "I knowed of a McQueen, right salty. He rid for John Chisum."

"Could be," McQueen admitted softly. "Where you from?"

Baldy looked up out of wise eyes. "Animas. Rid with 'Curly Bill' some, but I ain't no rustler no more. I left the owlhoot."

Red Naify was walking back. He looked at Ward thoughtfully.

"Yuh tired?" he asked suddenly. "I been workin' these boys pretty regular. How's about you night-herdin'?"

"Uh-huh." McQueen got up and stretched. "I didn't

come far today. No use a man ridin' the legs off his hoss when he ain't got to get noplace particular."

Naify chuckled. "That's right."

Ward McQueen saddled up and rode out toward the herd. He was very thoughtful. There seemed not a thing wrong, and yet he couldn't help feeling that something was very wrong. He shook his head. Baldy Jackson might or might not be off the owlhoot, but there was someone around whom Baldy didn't trust.

Idly, he let the roan circle the herd, bringing a few straying steers closer to the main herd. There was plenty of grass. It was a nice, comfortable spot to hole up for a few days.

Suddenly, an hour later, as the sun was just out of sight, he had an idea. He picked one of the steers away from the herd and, riding in, roped it. In a matter of seconds the young steer was tied. With a bit of stick he dug into the dirt on one hoof. A few minutes of examination, and he got up and turned the steer loose. It struggled erect and hiked back to the herd.

Ward McQueen mounted again, his face thoughtful. That critter had never crossed the alkali desert! There was no caked alkali dust on the hoof, none of it in the hair on the animal's leg. Wherever the cattle had come from, it hadn't been across the vast, salt plain where animals sank to their knees in the ashy waste. They had traveled in fairly good country, which meant they had come down from the north.

There was three hundred head of prime beef here, and it had been moved through pretty good country.

It was almost two o'clock in the morning and he had started back toward the camp when he saw the lean height of young Bud Fox walking toward him. He spotted him in the moonlight and reined in, waiting.

"How's it go?" Bud asked cheerfully. "I woke up and

thought maybe yuh'd like some coffee?" He held up a cup and held another for himself.

McQueen swung down and ground-hitched the roan.

"Tastes mighty good!" he said, after a pull at the coffee. He glanced up at Bud. "How long you and Baldy been with this herd?"

"Not long," Bud said. "We joined 'em here, too. We was ridin' down from the Blue Mountains, up Oregon way. Hoyt and Naify was already here. Said they'd been here a couple of days. Had two punchers when they come, they told us, but the punchers quit and headed for Montana."

"Yuh ever punch cows in Montana?" McQueen asked.

"Nope. Not me."

McQueen watched Bud walk back to camp and then forked the roan and started off, walking the horse. The stories of Baldy and Bud sounded straight enough. Baldy was admittedly from New Mexico and Arizona. Bud Fox said he had never ridden in Montana, and he looked like a southern rider. On the other hand, Red Naify, the foreman, who said he had driven in from Wyoming, rode a big horse and carried a thick, hemp lariat. Both were more typical of Montana cowhands.

It was almost daylight when McQueen heard the shot.

He had rounded the herd and was nearing the willows when the sudden *spang* of a rifle stabbed the stillness.

The one shot, then silence.

Touching spurs to the roan, he whipped it through the willows to the camp. Red Naify was standing, pistol in hand, at the edge of the firelight, staring into the darkness.

Both Baldy and Bud were sitting up in their blankets, and Baldy had his rifle in his hand.

"Where'd that shot come from?" McQueen demanded.

"Up on the mountain. It was some distance off," Naify said.

"Sounded close by to me," Bud retorted. "I'da sworn it was right close up in them trees."

"It was up on the mountain," Naify growled. He looked around at McQueen. "Them cows all right?"

"Sure thing. I'll go back."

"Wait." Fox rolled out of his blankets. "I'll go out. You been out all night."

"We're movin' in a couple of hours," Red Naify said. "You two will do the drivin'. Let him go back."

Ward McQueen turned the roan and rode back to the herd. It was not yet daylight. He could see the campfire flickering through the trees.

The herd was quiet. Some of the cattle had started up at the shot, but the stillness had quieted them again. Most of them were bedded down. With a quick glance toward the fire, McQueen turned the roan toward the mountain.

Skirting some clumps of piñon and juniper, he rode into the trees. It was gray, and the ground could be seen, but not well. He knew what he was looking for. If there had been a man, there must have been a horse. Perhaps the shot had been a miss. In any event, there had been no sound of movement in the stillness that followed. The roan's ears were keen, and he had given no indication of hearing anything.

He was riding through a clump of mazanita when he heard a horse stamp. He caught his own horse's nose, then ground-hitched it, and walked through the trees.

It was a fine-looking black horse, all of sixteen hands high, with a silver-mounted saddle. A Winchester '73 was in the scabbard, and the saddlebags were hand-tooled leather.

Working away from the horse, McQueen started toward the edge of the woods. He was still well under cover when he saw the dark outline of the body. He

31

glanced around, listened, then moved closer. He knelt in the gray dimness of dawn. The man was dead.

He was a young man, dressed in neat, expensive black. He wore one gun and it was in its holster. Gently, McQueen rolled the man on his back. He had been handsome as well as young, with a refined, sensitive face. Not, somehow, a Western face.

Slipping his hand inside the man's coat, McQueen withdrew a flat wallet. On it, in neat gold lettering, was the name *Dan Kermitt.* Inside, there was a sheaf of bills and other papers.

Suddenly McQueen heard a light footstep. Quickly, he slid the wallet into his shirt and stood up. Red Naify was standing on the edge of the woods.

"Looks like somebody got who he was shootin' at," McQueen drawled quietly. "Know him?"

Naify walked forward on cat feet. He looked down, then he shrugged.

"Never saw him afore!" He looked up, his piglike eyes gleaming. It was light enough now for McQueen to see their change of expression. "Did you kill him?"

"Me?" For an instant McQueen was startled. "No. I never saw this hombre before."

"Yuh could've," Red said, insinuatingly. "There wasn't nobody to see."

"So could you," McQueen said quietly. "So could you!"

"I got an alibi." Red grinned suddenly. "What the devil? I don't care who killed him. Injuns, probably. Find anythin' on him?"

"Never looked," McQueen replied carefully. How much had Red seen?

Naify stooped over the body and fanned it with swift, skillful fingers. In the right-hand pocket he found a small wallet containing a few bills and some gold coin. Ward McQueen stared at it thoughtfully, and when Naify straightened, he asked a question.

"Anythin' to tell who he was?"

"Not a thing. I'll jest keep this until somebody calls for it." He pocketed the money. "Yuh want to bury him?"

"Yeah. I'll bury him." McQueen stared down at the body. This was no place to bury a nice young man like this. But then, the West did strange things to people, bringing a strange grave to many a man.

"Hey." Red paused. "He should have a hoss. I better have a look around."

"Leave it to me," McQueen said quietly. "You got the money. I already found the hoss."

Red Naify hesitated, and for an instant his face was harsh and cruel. McQueen watched him, waiting. It was coming, sooner or later, and it could be now as well as later.

Naify shrugged, and started to turn away, then looked back. "Was it—the hoss, I mean—a big black?"

"Yeah," McQueen told him, unsmiling. "So yuh did know him?"

Naify's face darkened. "No. Only I seen somebody follerin' us that was ridin' a big black. Could've been him." He strode off toward camp.

Carrying the young man to a wash in the steep bank, he placed the body on the bottom, then caved dirt over it.

"Not much of a grave, friend," he said softly, "but I'll come back an' do her proper." He turned and as he walked away he added quietly, "And when I do, amigo, yuh can rest easy."

Standing in the brush near the black horse, he took out the flat leather wallet and opened it. He thrust his hand inside, then gulped in amazement. He was staring down at a sheaf of thousand-dollar bills!

Swiftly, he counted. Twenty-five of them, all new and crisp. There were two letters and a few odds and ends of no importance. He opened one letter, in feminine handwriting. It was short and to the point.

We have gone ahead to Fort Mallock. Come there with the money, as Kim has located a good ranch. I don't know what we'd have done without Iver, however, as ever since Father was killed, he has advised and helped me. The cattle are coming west with two of the most trustworthy hands, Chuck and Stan Jones.

Ruth

Replacing the wallet in his shirt, Ward McQueen swung into the saddle. He rode the black horse back to where his own horse waited, then leading his horse, he rode back to the camp.

Red Naify looked up at him, and then glanced at the horse, envy and greed shining in his eyes. Baldy looked up, too, and his eyes narrowed a little, but he said nothing. Bud Fox was already bunching the herd to start them moving.

Naify mounted up and joined him while McQueen ate. Twice he glanced up from his food to Baldy.

"Say," he said finally, "where was Red when yuh first looked up after that shot?"

"Red?" Baldy looked up, and put his big red hands on his hips. "Red wasn't in sight. Then I looked around, and he was standin' there. He could've been there all the time, but I don't think he was."

McQueen nodded up the hillside. "There was a dead man up there. He'd been lookin' us over from the cover of the trees. Right nice-lookin' gent. No rustler."

"Yuh think somebody's pullin' a steal?" Baldy asked shrewdly, stowing away the camp gear in the chuck wagon.

"Don't you?" Ward said quietly.

"Uh-huh. So what happens?" Baldy asked.

"My guess would be they don't intend to let us have no part of the profits. To us, the deal is supposed to be on the level. We don't know that it ain't," he added. "Actually, we don't know a thing."

34

"Uh-huh." Baldy crawled up on the wagon, and Mc-Queen tossed his now empty coffee cup into the back of the chuck wagon. "So we keep our eyes peeled, huh?"

"And a six-shooter handy," McQueen agreed grimly.

He tied the black horse to the wagon, then swung aboard the roan as the chuck wagon rumbled out after the cattle. McQueen started the roan after the herd at a canter, scowling thoughtfully.

The letter had referred to two trusted hands, Chuck and Stan Jones. Trusted men didn't ride away and leave a herd. Not to go back to Montana or anywhere. What had happened to them, then? Where were they?

The trail wound slowly up toward the pass in the Toana range. The cattle moved slowly, reluctant to leave the green meadows bordering Pilot Creek. There was little time for thinking as two old steers had no intention of leaving the creek and made break after break trying to get away.

Late in the afternoon, Bud Fox rode up beside Mc-Queen. He lighted a smoke, then glanced across the herd at Naify.

"Nice hoss yuh got back there," he commented casually. "Hombre what owned him's dead, I s'pose?"

"Uh-huh. I buried him. A darned good rifle shot killed him."

Bud rode quietly. "Yuh know," he said softly, "I been wonderin' a mite. When Baldy and me come up the trail, we got us a glimpse of somethin'. Way north of where we was, but on the Montana trail. We seen us some buzzards circlin'—like maybe a dead critter was lyin' there."

"Or dead men." Ward McQueen's voice was grim. "Men who might object to what was goin' to be done with these cows."

"Uh-huh," Fox agreed, "like that. Or maybe riders the boss didn't have no intention of payin'. On a long drive, yuh know, ain't nobody goin' to be surprised if a cowpoke never comes back. He could've gone on to

Californy, or maybe south of the Colorado country. Or he could've just started driftin'."

The herd moved steadily westward, camping one night at Flower Lake, a grass-covered and spring-fed swamp, then moving on up the steep slopes of the Pequops through a scattered forest of mountain mahogany, juniper, and piñon. Ward McQueen, his battered gray hat pulled low over his gray eyes, his lean-jawed face ever more quiet, ever more watchful.

Red Naify held to the point, rarely leaving it even for a few minutes. The blocky, hard-faced foreman rode cautiously, and once, when they sighted several horsemen, he let the herd veer southward, away from them.

On the west side of the Pequops the herd ambled slowly across a sage-covered valley toward the distant violet and purple of mountains, and finally, almost in the shadow of the Humboldt Range, the herd was circled for a night stop on the edge of Snow Water Lake.

Naify rode back. "Bed 'em down here," he said. "We'll spend the night and let 'em feed some more. No use losin' too much beef on this move."

"Where's Mallock?" McQueen asked suddenly.

Naify turned his head and looked squarely at him. "Don't worry about it. We ain't goin' near Mallock!"

Thoughtfully, Ward watched Red ride away. Red Naify knew nothing of the letter in McQueen's pocket. In that simple statement he had given himself away. The girl was waiting at Fort Mallock for the cattle. Iver Hoyt was probably with her. He was the trusted adviser, and he was stealing her herd!

In McQueen's pocket, given him by a friend before he ever started for this country, was a map. It showed Mallock, the fort built only a short time before, to be not far beyond the Humboldt Mountains. He made a sudden decision.

Wheeling his horse, he rode to the chuck wagon, where Baldy had unhitched the team. The cattle were drinking, and Bud Fox was sitting his horse nearby, rolling a smoke.

"Listen," he said, reining in the roan beside the wagon. "I'm ridin' out of here. I got me an idea. You two better keep plenty close watch. I figger this is where she happens!"

Fox nodded. "Red said he'd be back sometime tomorrow or the day after. That we was to sit tight. Where yuh goin'?"

"Fort Mallock. I'm ridin' the black."

It was dark when the black horse cantered down the dusty street of the little community that had grown up around the Fort. Ward McQueen rode up to the hitching rail and swung down. He hitched his belt and loosened his guns. He had just stepped up on the walk when a wiry, broad-shouldered man stepped out from the batwing doors.

For an instant the man stood stock-still, his eyes on the black horse, then his eyes shifted to McQueen.

"Yore hoss, podner?" he queried gently.

McQueen felt something inside him tighten. There was something in the faint suggestion of that voice that warned him. This man was dangerous.

"I'm ridin' him," he replied quietly.

"Where'd yuh get him?" the stranger asked, stepping away from in front of the door.

"Before I answer that," McQueen said quietly, "s'pose yuh tell me why yuh ask and who yuh are."

The young man stared back at him, and McQueen decided there was something in the black eyes and brown, young face that he liked.

"My name," the young man said evenly, "is Kim Sartain. And the man who owned that hoss, and that saddle, was a friend of mine!"

"So yuh're Kim," McQueen said softly. "Yuh know an hombre name of Iver Hoyt?"

Sartain's face darkened and his eyes grew cautious. "Yeah, I know him. A friend of yores?"

"No." McQueen looked at him thoughtfully. "Yuh know where Ruth Kermitt is?"

"Yeah."

"Then take me to her. I'll talk there."

Leading the black horse, Ward McQueen followed Kim. The young man walked alongside him, his left side toward McQueen, who grinned to himself at this precaution.

"Yuh don't take no chances, Sartain," he said. "But I think we're on the same side."

Kim's hard face did not relent. "I'll know that when yuh tell me where yuh got that hoss."

McQueen tied the horse to a hitching rail, followed Sartain into a small hotel, and into a back parlor, a small, comfortably furnished room. There was a girl sitting on the divan, and she rose quickly when they came in.

McQueen halted, his face suddenly blank. He had expected anything but the tall, lovely girl who faced him. Probably twenty years old, she was erect, poised, and lovely, her black hair gathered in a loose knot at the nape of her neck, her blue eyes wide.

Kim spoke, his voice flat. "This hombre hones to talk with yuh, ma'am. He rode into town on Dan's hoss."

"Ma'am," McQueen said quietly, "I'm afraid I'm bringin' bad news."

"It's Dan! Something's happened to Dan!" Ruth Kermitt came toward him quickly. "What is it? Please tell me now!"

McQueen's face flushed, then paled a little. "He's— he's been killed, ma'am. Shot!"

Her face turned deathly white, and she fell back a step, her eyes still wide. Swiftly, Kim crossed to her side.

"Ma'am," he said. "Better hold yoreself together. We

got to get this hombre's yarn. He may need killin' hisself." He spoke this last in a low, dangerous tone.

Briefly, with no details, McQueen explained, saying nothing about the herd except to mention the names of the men riding with it.

Kim stared at him. "A herd of three hundred whitefaces? And *with Red Naify*? Who're those others yuh mentioned?"

"Baldy Jackson and Bud Fox. Good men. Naify told us the other riders rode off and left 'em."

"Like the devil they did!" Kim snapped. "Somebody's lyin', ma'am!"

"We'd better get Iver," Ruth said hesitantly. "He always knows what to do."

Ward McQueen shook his head. "If yuh mean Iver Hoyt, ma'am, I wouldn't get him. He's a crook, tryin' to rustle them cattle hisself."

Ruth stiffened and her eyes flashed.

"You don't know what you're saying!" she said sharply. "He's been a very good friend! My only friend, aside from Kim here. And *he* wasn't found riding Dan's horse!"

"I reckon not," McQueen replied grimly, "but he—"

The door opened suddenly to interrupt him, and Iver Hoyt stepped in, two men crowding in behind him.

"Ruth!" he said, "Dan's horse is outside!" His eyes found Ward McQueen and his lips tightened. "Ruth, who is this man?"

"Don't yuh remember me?" McQueen said gently. "That Texas rider yuh hired back at Pilot Creek. The one yuh told Red Naify to work on the same basis as the others."

"Yuh're crazy!" Hoyt snapped. "I never saw yuh before in my life. As for Red Naify, the man's an outlaw! A rustler!"

"If I never saw yuh before," McQueen said quietly, "how do I know yore gun butt's got the head of a longhorn steer on it? How do I know yuh ride a bay hoss with three white stockin's?"

Kim stood with his thumbs hooked in his belt. "I've noticed that steer's head, Hoyt. And he sure enough has yore hoss spotted."

"He's a liar!" Hoyt snarled, his hands poised. "I never saw him before!"

"I'll take care of that liar business in due time," McQueen said softly. "In the meantime, tell us what happened to Chuck and Stan Jones!"

Ruth looked up quickly, staring at Hoyt. Iver Hoyt's face tightened.

"They went back to Montana!" he snapped.

"They were coming on here, Iver," Ruth Kermitt said quietly. "Yuh know they'd promised to work for me. They wouldn't break a promise. Neither of them would."

Hoyt stiffened and his eyes turned hard. "So? You don't believe me either? We'll discuss this in the mornin'!" He turned abruptly and walked from the room, followed by the two men with him.

"Ma'am, I think I better get back to them cattle," Ward McQueen suggested suddenly. "Hoyt'll try to steal 'em, and soon. In fact, I think he'll try it sooner now than he'd planned."

"I'll go back with yuh," Kim said. "I think yuh're smokin' some skunks out of this tree, podner!"

It was almost daylight when they rode down the slope of the mountain near Secret Pass and cut across the plain toward Snow Water. They were still almost a half mile away when a volley of shots rang out.

McQueen touched spurs to the black and whipped it around some tall sage and started on a dead run for the camp. Then, ahead, there was another shot. Then another and another.

He sighted the wagon and slowed down. Kim Sartain was behind him, and suddenly McQueen glimpsed the moonlight on Baldy's head. At the same instant he saw the gleam of a lifted rifle.

"Hold it!" he yelled. "It's me!"

He swung down. "What happened?"

Baldy grinned. "After yuh left, we got to thinkin', so when it come dark we rolled up some sacks and left them on the ground near the fire. Then we moved back in the sagebrush. A few minutes ago some rannies come up and let go with a volley into those dummies. A half minute later I see one of 'em move closer for a look, and I let him have it."

Suddenly a voice called out of the darkness. "Hey, Baldy!" It was Red Naify calling. "Put down yore guns. It's all right. They run off when they saw me and the boss comin'."

McQueen fell back into the deep shadows under the wagon.

"Get out of sight, Kim," he whispered. "They didn't see us come in. Call 'em in, Baldy, but be careful."

At that moment there was a soft voice from the shadows in the direction Ward and Sartain had come.

"I'm going to wait here. I want to see this, too."

It was Ruth Kermitt! She had followed them out from town. Well, maybe it was the best way, McQueen thought.

"Come on in," Baldy said, "but come slow."

Red Naify, his blocky, powerful body looking even bigger in the dancing firelight, came first. After him, only a step behind but to the right, was Iver Hoyt.

"Glad yuh boys ain't turned in yet," Red said. "We're goin' to move these cows."

"Tonight?" Baldy objected. "Where to?"

"Up in the Humboldts," Hoyt said. "I know the place." He looked around. "Who was shootin'?"

"That's what we wondered." Bud Fox had his thumbs in his gun belt. His eyes shifted from Naify to Hoyt. "Lucky they didn't get us."

Ward, crouching under the wagon, could see what was coming. Naify had casually moved two steps farther

41

to the left. Baldy and Bud were going to be caught in a cross fire. He stepped from under the wagon and straightened, hearing Kim move out also.

One step took him into the firelight. "Fall back, you two," he said quietly. "I'm takin' over!"

"And me," Kim said. "Don't forget me."

"Yuh're an awful fool, Hoyt," Ward McQueen said suddenly. "Why don't yuh ask Naify what he did with the money he took off Dan Kermitt."

Hoyt's eyes suddenly blazed up. "Naify, did yuh get that fifty thousand?"

"*Fifty thousand?*" Stark incredulity rang in Red Naify's voice. "Why, I only got sixty dollars!" Suddenly his eyes gleamed. "Boss, *he's* got it! He's got it right there in his pocket!"

Iver Hoyt smiled suddenly. "So, we won't lose after all! Boys, come in!"

There was a sound of movement, and four more men stepped into the circle of light. One of them tossed a bundle of brush on the fire, and it blazed up.

"Think yuh're pretty smart, don't yuh, Hoyt?" McQueen said quietly. "Yuh engineered this whole steal, didn't yuh?"

"Of course," Hoyt admitted proudly. "We stole old Kermitt blind up in Montana. He was too fresh from the East to know what was happenin' to him. Then he found us that night and I had to kill him."

Suddenly a new voice sounded. "You four back up against the wagon and stay out of this. I've got a double-barrel shotgun here, and if there is one move out of you, I'll let you have both barrels!"

Ruth Kermitt stood there. Tall, splendid in the firelight, she looked like a portrait of all the pioneer women of any age. The shotgun she held was steady and she waved the four back.

"I'll second that motion, ma'am," Bud Fox said quietly, "with a six-gun!"

Baldy spoke suddenly and his voice drawled.

"This is goin' to be pretty. Real pretty," he said. "Hoyt, yuh know who this ranny is yuh're talkin' to? This here's Ward McQueen. Think back a ways. Where'd yuh hear that name afore?"

Baldy paused, and he saw a frown appear on Iver Hoyt's face.

"Ward, yuh had a bosom friend in Larry White, didn't yuh?" he said to McQueen then. "Well, Iver Hoyt's full name is Iver Hoyt Harris!"

"*Ike Harris!*" Ward McQueen's face suddenly went stone cold. "Kim," he said suddenly, and his voice rang loud, "as a favor, let me have them both! *Now!*"

It was Hoyt who moved first. At the mention of Larry White's name, his face went dead pale, and his hand, twitching nervously, shot down for his gun.

McQueen's six-guns seemed to leap from their holsters, spewing jagged darts of fire. Hoyt, caught full in the chest by a leaden slug, was smashed back to his heels, and then another slug caught him in the face, and another in the throat.

Coolly, ignoring Red Naify, he poured fire into the killer of his friend. Then he took one swinging step, bringing himself around to face Naify.

Red, a leer on his face, was waiting.

"Yuh dirty coyote!" he snarled.

Both men's guns belched flame. Red swayed on his feet, and then Ward McQueen stepped forward, firing as coolly as though on a target range. He stepped again, and each time his foot planted, his guns roared. Smashed back by the heavy slugs Red Naify staggered, then toppled to his knees.

His face a bloody mess from a bullet that had burned a hole through the right side of his face below the eye, he lifted his gun and fired again. The bullet hit McQueen and he staggered, but bracing himself, he brought one gun down and triggered it again. The dart of fire seemed almost to touch Red's face, and he toppled over on his face in the dust, his gun belching one last grass-cutting shot as his fist closed in agony.

Ward McQueen staggered a little and then, stooping with great care, picked up his hat.

"The devil," he said, "only three bullet holes! Wyatt Earp had five after his battle with Curly Bill's gang at the water hole."

Ruth Kermitt ran to his side. "You're hurt! Oh, you're hurt!" she exclaimed.

He turned to look at her, and then suddenly everything faded out.

When he opened his eyes again it was morning. Ruth sat beside him, her eyes heavy with weariness. She put a cool cloth on his forehead and wiped his face off with another.

"You must lie still," she told him. "You've lost a lot of blood."

"Of course, if yuh say so, ma'am," he assured her. "I'll lay right quiet."

Baldy Jackson looked at him and snorted.

"Look at that, would yuh!" he exploded. "And that's the ranny crawled three miles with seven holes in him after his Galeyville fight! Just goes to show yuh what a woman'll do to a man!"

When a Texan Takes Over

When Matt Ryan saw the cattle tracks on Mocking Bird, he swung his horse over under the trees and studied the terrain with a careful eye. For those cattle tracks meant rustlers were raiding the KY range.

For a generation the big KY spread had been the law in the Slumbering Hill country, but now the old man was dying and the wolves were coming out of the breaks to tear at the body of the ranch.

And there was nobody to stop them, nobody to step into the big tracks old Tom Hitch had made, nobody to keep law in the hills now that old Tom was dying. He had built an empire of land cattle, but he had also brought law into the outlaw country, brought schools and a post office, and the beginnings of thriving settlement.

But they had never given up, not Indian Kelly nor Lee Dunn. They'd waited back in the hills, bitter with their own poison, waiting for the old man to die.

All the people in the Slumbering Hill country knew it, and they had looked to Fred Hitch, the old man's adopted son, to take up the job when the old man put it down. But Fred was an easygoing young man who liked to drink and gamble. And he spent too much time with Dutch Gerlach, the KY foreman . . . and who had a good word for Dutch?

"This is the turn, Red," Ryan told his horse. "They know the old man will never ride again, so they have started rustling."

It was not just a few head . . . there must have been forty or more in this bunch, and no attempt to cover the trail.

In itself that was strange. It seemed they were not even worried about what Gerlach might do . . . and what would he do? Dutch Gerlach was a tough man. He had shown it more than once. Of course, nobody wanted any part of Lee Dunn, not even Gerlach.

Matt Ryan rode on, but kept a good background behind him. He had no desire to skyline himself with rustlers around.

For three months now he had been working his placer claim in Pima Canyon, just over the ridge from Mocking Bird. He had a good show of color and with persistent work he made better than cowhand's wages. But lately he was doing better. Twice in the past month he had struck pockets that netted him nearly a hundred dollars each. The result was that his last month had brought him in the neighborhood of three hundred in gold.

Matt Ryan knew the hills and the men who rode them. None of them knew him. Matt had a streak of Indian in his nature if not in his blood, and he knew how to leave no trail and travel without being seen. He was around, but not obvious.

They knew somebody was there, but who and why or where they did not know, and he liked it that way. Once a month he came out of the hills for supplies, but he never rode to the same places. Only this time he was coming back to Hanna's Stage Station. He told himself it was because it was close, but down inside he knew it was because of Kitty Hanna.

She was something who stepped out of your dreams, a lovely girl of twenty in a cotton dress and with carefully done hair, large, dark eyes, and a mouth that would set a man to being restless. . . .

Matt Ryan had stopped by two months before to eat a woman-cooked meal and to buy supplies, and he had lingered over his coffee.

He was a tall, wide-shouldered young man with a slim, long-legged body and hands that swung wide of his narrow hips. He had a wedge-shaped face and green eyes, and a way of looking at you with faint humor in his eyes.

He carried a gun, but he carried it tucked into his waistband, and he carried a Winchester that he never left on his saddle.

Nobody knew him around the Slumbering Hills, nobody knew him anywhere this side of Texas . . . they remembered him there. His name was a legend on the Nueces.

Big Red ambled on down the trail and Matt watched the country and studied the cattle tracks. He would remember those horse tracks, too. Finally the cow tracks turned off into a long valley, and when he sat his horse he could see dust off over there where Thumb Butte lifted against the sky.

Indian Kelly . . . not Dunn this time, although Dunn might have given the word.

Kitty was pouring coffee when he came in and she felt her heart give a tiny leap. It had only been once, but she remembered, for when his eyes touched her that time, it made her feel the woman in her . . . a quick excitement such as she felt now.

Why was that? This man whom she knew nothing about? Why should he make her feel this way?

He put his hat on a hook and sat down, and she saw that his hair was freshly combed and still damp from the water he had used. That meant he had stopped back there by the creek . . . it was unlike a drifting cowhand, or had it been for her?

When he looked up she knew it had, and she liked the smile he had and the way his eyes could not seem to leave her face. "Eggs," he said, "about four of them, and whatever vegetable you have, and a slab of beef. I'm a hungry man."

She filled his cup, standing very close to him, and she saw the red mount under his dark skin, and when she moved away it was slowly, and there was a little something in her walk. Had her father seen it, he would have been angry, but this man would not be angry, and he would know it was for him.

Dutch Gerlach came in, a big, brawny man with bold eyes and careless hands. He had a wide, flat face and a confident, knowing manner that she hated. Fred Hitch was with him.

They looked at Ryan, then looked again. He was that sort of man, and something about him irritated Gerlach. But the big foreman of the KY said nothing. He was watching Kitty.

Gerlach seated himself and shoved his hat back on his head. When his meal was put before him, he began to eat, his eyes following the girl. Fred seemed preoccupied; he kept scowling a little, and he said something under his breath to Dutch.

Gerlach looked over at Matt Ryan. "Ain't seen you around before," he said.

Ryan merely glanced at him, and continued eating. The eggs tasted good, and the coffee was better than his own.

"Hear what I said?" Gerlach demanded.

Ryan looked up, studying the bigger man calmly. "Yes," he said, "and the remark didn't require an answer."

Gerlach started to speak, then devoted himself to his food.

"That bay horse yours?" Fred Hitch asked suddenly.

Ryan nodded . . . they had seen the horse, then? That was one trouble with Big Red, he was a blood bay, and he stood out. It would have been better to have a dun or a buckskin . . . even a black.

"It's mine," he said.

Yet their curiosity and Fred's uneasiness puzzled him. Why should Fred be bothered by him?

"Don't take to strangers around here," Gerlach said suddenly. "You move on."

Ryan said nothing, although he felt something inside of him grow poised and waiting. No trouble, Matt, he warned himself, not here . . .

"Hear me?" Gerlach's voice rose. "We've missed some cows."

Kitty had come to the door, and her father was behind her. Hanna was a peace-loving man, but a stern one.

"I heard you," Ryan replied quietly, "an' if you've missed cows, ride toward Thumb Butte."

Fred Hitch jerked as if he had been slapped, and Gerlach's face went slowly dark. His eyes had been truculent, now they were cautious, studying. "What's that mean?" he asked, his voice low.

"Ain't that where Indian Kelly hangs out?" Ryan asked mildly.

"You seem to know." Gerlach was suddenly cold. "I figure you're a rustler your own self!"

It was fighting talk, gun talk. Matt Ryan made no move. He forked up some more eggs. "One man's opinion," he said. "But what would make you think that? You've never seen me with a rope on my saddle, you've never even seen me before. You don't know where I'm from or where I'm going."

All this was true. . . . Gerlach hesitated, wanting trouble, yet disturbed by the other man's seeming calm.

He had no gun in sight, and his rifle leaned against the wall. Still, you couldn't tell.

He snorted and sat down, showing his contempt for a man who would take an insult without fighting, yet he was uneasy.

Matt glanced up to meet Kitty's eyes. She turned her face deliberately, and he flushed. She thought him a coward.

He lingered over his coffee, wanting a word with her, and finally the others left. He looked up when the door closed behind them. "There's a dance at Rock Springs," he said suddenly. "Would you go with me?"

She hesitated, then stiffened a little. "I'd be afraid to," she said. "Somebody might call you a coward in front of people."

Scarcely were the words out than she was sorry she had said them. His face went white and she felt a queer little pang and half turned toward him. He got up slowly, his face very stiff. Then he walked to the door. There he turned. "You find it so easy to see a man die?" he asked, and the words were shocking in their tone and in the something that spoke from his eyes.

He went out, and the door closed, and Hanna said, to his daughter, "I don't want you speakin' to men like that. Nor do I want you goin' dancin' with strangers. Just the same," he added, "I'd say that man was not afraid."

She thought about it and her father's words remained with her. She held them tenderly, for she wanted to believe in them, yet she had seen the stranger take a deliberate insult without a show of resentment. Men had killed for less. Of course, she had not wanted that. (How he could have shown resentment without its leading to bloodshed she did not ask herself.)

She was at the window when he rode out of town, and was turning away from it when the side door opened and a slender, narrow-faced man stood there. She felt a start of fear. This was not the first time she had seen Lee Dunn, and there was something about him that frightened her.

"Who was that?" he demanded. "That man who walked out?"

"I . . . I don't know," she said, and then was surprised to realize that it was the truth. She knew nothing about him, and she had seen him but twice.

Lee Dunn was a narrow, knifelike man with a bitter mouth that never smiled, but there was a certain arresting quality about him so that even when you knew who and what he was, you respected him. His manner was old-fashioned and courteous, but without graciousness. It was rumored that he had killed a dozen men . . . and he had killed two here at the Springs.

Kitty rode to the party in a buckboard with Fred Hitch. And she was dancing her third dance when she looked up and saw the stranger standing at the floor's edge. He wore a dark red shirt that was freshly laundered and a black string tie. There was a short jacket of buckskin, Mexican style, over the shirt. His black boots were freshly polished.

She saw Dutch Gerlach watching him, and was aware of worry that there would be trouble. Yet two dances passed, one of them with Dutch, whom she hated but could not avoid without one dance, and he did not come near her. Someone mentioned his name. Matt Ryan . . . she liked the sound.

Lee Dunn came into the room and paused near Gerlach. She thought she saw Dutch's lips move, but he did not turn his head. But that was silly . . . why would the foreman of the KY talk to a rustler?

When she looked again Matt Ryan was gone . . . and he had not even asked her for a dance.

Something seemed to have gone from the lights, and her feet lost their quickness. Suddenly, she knew she wanted to go home. . . .

•   •   •

Matt Ryan was riding fast. He had seen Dunn come into the room and turned at once and slipped out through the crowd. What was to be done had to be done fast, and he went at it.

The big bay was fast, and he held the pace well. An hour after leaving the dance Ryan swung the big horse into the KY ranch yard and got down. With only a glance at the darkened bunkhouse he crossed to the big house and went in.

He had not stopped to knock, and he startled the big Mexican woman who was dusting a table. "Where's Tom?" he demanded.

"You can't see him." The woman barred his way, her fat face growing hard. "He sick."

"I'll see him. Show me to him."

"I'll not! You stop or I'll—"

"Maria!" The voice was a husky roar. "Who's out there?"

Matt Ryan walked by her to the bedroom doorway. He stopped there, looking in at the old man.

Tom Hitch had been a giant. He was a shell now, bedridden and old, but with a flare of ancient fire in his eyes.

"You don't know me, Hitch," Ryan said, "but it's time you did. You're losin' cattle."

Before the old man could speak, Ryan broke in, talking swiftly. He told about forty head that had left the day before, in broad daylight. He told of other, smaller herds. He told of the rustlers' growing boldness, of Lee Dunn at the dance, of Indian Kelly riding down to Hanna's Stage Station.

"They wouldn't dare!" The old man's voice was heavy with scorn. "I learnt 'em manners!"

"And now you're abed," Matt Ryan said roughly. "And you've a fool and an outlaw for an adopted son, a gunman for a foreman."

Hitch was suddenly quiet. His shrewd old eyes studied Ryan. "What's in you, man? What d' you want?"

"You're down, Hitch. Maybe you'll get up, maybe not. But what happens to the country? What happens to law an' order when—"

Somebody moved behind him and he turned to see Fred Hitch standing there with Dutch Gerlach. Fred was frightened, but there was ugliness in the foreman's face.

"You invite this gent here?" Dutch asked thickly.

"No." Old Tom sat up a little. "Tell him to get out and stay out."

The old man hunched his pillow behind him. "He forced his way in here with some cock-an'-bull story about rustlin'."

Gerlach looked at Ryan and jerked his head toward the door. "You heard him. Get *out!*"

Matt Ryan walked to the door and went down the steps. Then swiftly he turned the corner and ran for his horse. A rifle shot slammed the darkness and knocked a chip from a tree trunk, but his turn had been sudden and unexpected. He hit the saddle running and the bay bounded like a rabbit and was gone into the darkness under the trees. A second and a third shot wasted themselves in the night.

How had they gotten on his trail so suddenly? They must have left the dance almost as soon as he had. And where was Kitty Hanna?

Miles fell behind him, and the trail was abandoned for the sidehills and trees, and he worked his way across ridges and saddles, and found himself back at Pima Canyon with the sun coming up.

All was still below, and he watched for half an hour before going down. When he got there he packed his spare horse and rode out of the canyon, leaving his diggings. They were good and getting better, but no place for him now. There were too many marks of his presence.

Why had he gotten into this? It was no business of his. What if the lawless did come from the hills and the good times of the old KY were gone? Could he not ride on? He owned nothing here, he did not belong here. This was a problem for others, not himself. But was it?

Was not the problem of the law and of community peace the problem of all men? Could any safely abandon their right of choice to others? Might not their own shiftlessness rob them of all they valued?

Bedding down in the high pines under the stars, Matt Ryan thought himself to sleep over that. He had taken a foolish step into the troubles of others. He would stay out. Old Tom did not want his help, nor did Kitty want his love.

Two days he rode the hills, for two days shifting camp each night. For two days he was irritable. It was none of his business, he kept telling himself. The old man had sent him packing, Kitty had turned him down. Nevertheless, he could not settle down. He rode back to Pima Canyon and looked around.

Their tracks were everywhere. They had found this place, and had without doubt come looking for him. So he was a hunted man now. It was good to know.

Yet he did not leave. Without reason for remaining, he remained.

And on the third day he rode to Hanna's Station. Kitty was not there, but her father was. Hanna looked at him carefully. "Maria huntin' you. Come in here ridin' a mule. Acted like she didn't aim to be seen. Left word you was to see her."

"All right," he said.

Hanna brought him coffee and a meal. "Ain't Kitty's grub," he said. "She's to town."

The older man sat down. Dutch Gerlach was in with two men, he told Ryan, hunting for him. Or maybe, he added, hunting Fred Hitch.

"Hitch?"

"He's gone. Dropped out of sight. Nobody knows why."

A rattle of horses' hooves sounded and Matt Ryan

came to his feet quickly. Outside were four men. Dutch Gerlach, two hands . . . and Lee Dunn.

Ryan turned sharply. He had left his horse in the trees and there was a chance it had not been seen. Stepping into the kitchen, he moved back to a door on his right. He opened it and stepped through. He was in Kitty's room.

There was a stamp of boots outside and a distant sound of voices, then a rattle of dishes.

What had happened? If Lee Dunn and Gerlach were together, then—

Suddenly he was conscious of a presence. In the shadowed room he had seen nothing. Now his hand dropped to his gun and he started to turn.

"Don't shoot, Ryan. It's me. Hitch."

In a quick step Ryan was at the bedside. Fred Hitch lay in the bed, his face drawn and pale. His shoulder and arm were bandaged.

"It was them." He indicated the men outside. "Gerlach egged me into sellin' some of the KY cows for gamblin' money, said it would all be mine, anyway. Then he began sellin' some himself, dared me to tell the old man.

"Lee Dunn was in it with him, and I was scared. I went along, but I didn't like it. Then, when you saw the old man, they got worried. They couldn't find you, and they decided to kill the old man, then to take over. I wouldn't stand for it, and made a break. They shot me down, but I got to a horse. Kitty hid me here . . . she went after medicine."

"They'll wonder why she isn't here now," Ryan said half aloud. Then he looked down at the man on the bed. "What about Tom? Did they kill him?"

"Don't think so. They want me for a front . . . or him. Then they can loot the ranch safely. After that, other outfits."

Ryan stepped to the window. With luck he could make the trees without being seen. He put a hand on the window and slid it up.

"Ryan?"

"Yeah."

"I ain't much, but the old man was good to me. I wouldn't see no harm come to him. Tell him that, will you?"

"Sure."

He stepped out the window and walked swiftly into the woods. There he made the saddle and started for the KY. He had no plan, he had not even the right to plan. It was not his fight. He was a stranger and . . . but he kept riding.

It was past midnight when he found the KY. He had been lost for more than an hour, took a wrong trail in the bad light . . . there were no lights down below. He rode the big horse down through the trees and stepped out of the saddle.

There were a dozen saddled horses near the corral. He could see the shine of the starlight on the saddles. He saw some of those horses when he drew closer, and he knew them. They were riders from Thumb Butte . . . so, then, they had the ranch. They had moved in.

And this ranch was the law. There were no other forces to stand against Gerlach and Dunn now. There were ten thousand head of cattle in the hills, all to be sold. It was wealth, and a community taken over.

He stood there in the darkness, his face grim, smelling the night smells, feeling the danger and tension, knowing he was a fool to stay, yet unable to run.

The old man might still be alive. If he could move in, speak to him once more . . . with just the shadow of authority he might draw good men around him and hold the line. He was nobody now, but with the authority of old Tom Hitch, then he could move.

He loosened his gun in his belt, and taking his rifle walked across the clearing to the back door. He saw a

man come to the bunkhouse door and throw out a cigarette. The man started to turn, then stopped and looked
his way. He kept on walking, his mouth dry, his heart
pounding. The fellow watched him for a minute, barely
visible in the gloom, and then went back inside.

Matt Ryan reached the back of the house and touched the
latch. It lifted under his hand and he stepped in. Carefully, he eased across the room, into the hall. When he
made the old man's room, he hesitated, then spoke softly.
There was no reply.

He struck a match . . . it glowed, flared. Matt
looked at the old man, who was slumped back against the
headboard of his bed, his flannel nightshirt bloody, the
eyes wide and staring. They had murdered Tom Hitch.
Killed him without a chance.

Matt drew back, hearing a noise at the bunkhouse.
The match died and he dropped it, rubbing it out with his
toe.

A faint rustle behind him and he turned, gun in
hand.

A big old form loomed in the dark, wide, shapeless.
"It me . . . Maria. He say give you this." A paper rattled
and he took it. "You go . . . quick now."

He went swiftly, hearing boots grating on the gravel.
They were suspicious, and coming to look. He stepped
out the back door and a man rounded the corner. "Hey,
there!" the fellow started forward. "Wait . . . !"

Matt Ryan shot him. He held the gun low and he shot
at the middle of the man's body, and heard the other
man's gun blast muffled by his body.

He started by him, and a light flared somewhere
and its light caught the man's face. He had killed Indian
Kelly.

Rifle in hand, he ran, ducking into the trees. There
were shouts behind him, and he saw men scatter out,
coming. He could see their darker shapes against the gray

of the yard. He fired four fast shots from the hip, scattering them across the yard. A man stumbled and went
down, then the others hit the dirt.

He ran for the bay, caught the bridle reins, and
stepped into the leather. "Let's get out of here!" he said,
and the big red horse was moving . . . fast.

Day was graying when he neared Hanna's Station.
He saw no horses around, so he rode boldly from the
woods to the back door. In the gray of the light, he swung
down and knocked.

Kitty opened the door. He stepped in, grim, unshaven. "Got some coffee?" he said. "And I want to see
Fred."

"You . . . they killed him. Gerlach and Dunn. They
found him."

"Your father?"

"He's hurt . . . they knocked him out."

He looked at her hungrily, anxious to feel her need of
him. With his fingers he spread the paper Maria had
given him.

> *Matt Ryan: Take over.*
> *Tom Hitch*

The signature was big and sprawled out, but a signature known all over the Slumbering Hills.

So . . . there it was. The problem was his now.
Looking back, he could remember the old man's eyes.
Hitch had known that if he had shown the slightest will-
ingness to listen to Ryan, they would both have been
killed. But now the battle had been tossed to him.

Kitty looked at him, waiting. "There it is, Matt.
You're the boss of Slumbering Hills."

The boss . . . and a hunted man. His only supporters an old man with an aching head, and a girl.

One man alone . . . with a gun.

●　　●　　●

They would be combing the hills for him. They would come back here. Kitty had been left alone, but then they were in a hurry to find him and Tom Hitch was living. Now it would be different.

"Saddle up," he said. "You and your dad are riding. Ride to the ranches, get the men together."

"What about you?" Her eyes were very large. "Matt, what about you?"

"Me? I'll wait here."

"But they'll come here! They'll be looking for you."

"Uh-huh . . . so I show 'em who's boss." He grinned suddenly, boyishly. "Better rustle some help. They might not believe me."

When they had left, he waited. The stage station was silent, the throbbing heart gone from it. He poured coffee into a cup, remembering that it was up to him now. . . . Suppose . . . suppose he could do it without a gun. . . . A time had come for change, the old order was gone . . . but did Lee Dunn know that? And in his heart, Matt Ryan knew he did not. For Lee Dunn was the old order. He was a relic, a leftover, a memory of the days when Tom Hitch had come here, Hitch already past his prime, Dunn not yet to reach his. . . .

In the silent house the clock ticked loudly. Matt Ryan sipped his coffee and laid his Winchester on the table.

He checked his gun while the clock ticked off the measured seconds.

It was broad day now. . . . Kitty and her father would be well into the valley. Would the ranchers come? His was a new voice, they did not know him. They had only that slip of paper and the words *Take over*.

He got up and walked to the window. And then he saw them coming.

He placed his rifle by the door and stepped outside. There were ten of them . . . ten, and one of him. A fleeting smile touched his lips. Old Tom Hitch had stood off forty Apaches once . . . alone.

"Tom," he whispered, "if you can hear me . . . say a word where it matters."

He stepped to the edge of the porch, a tall man, honed down by sparse living and hard years, his wedge-shaped face unshaven, his eyes cool, waiting. It had been like this on the Nueces . . . only different.

They drew up, a line of men on horses. Lee Dunn and Gerlach at the center.

He saw no others, he thought of no others. These were the ones.

"Hello, Dunn."

The knifelike man studied him, his hands on the horn of his saddle.

"Dunn, I'm serving notice. Tom Hitch sent me a note. His orders were for me to take over."

"Think you can?"

"I can."

Lee Dunn waited . . . why he waited he could not have said. He had heard from Gerlach that this man was yellow. Looking at him, seeing him, he knew he was not. He knew another thing—this man was a gunfighter.

"Who are you, Ryan? Should I know you?"

"From the Nueces . . . maybe you heard of the Kenzie outfit."

Lee Dunn's lips thinned down. Of course . . . he should have known. It had been a feud . . . and at the last count there were five Kenzies and one Ryan left. And now there was still one Ryan . . .

"So this is the way it is," Matt said, making his plea. "The old days are over, Lee. You an' me, we're of the past. Old Tom was, too. He was a good man, and his guns kept the peace and made the law. But the old days of living by the gun are gone, Lee. We can admit it, or we can die."

"Where's the girl?" Gerlach demanded.

"Gone with her father. They are in the valley now

rounding up all of Old Tom's supporters from the Slumberin' Hills."

His eyes held on them, seeing them both, knowing them both. "What's it to be, Dunn?"

A voice spoke behind him. "I did not go. . . . Dad went. I'm here with a shotgun and I'm saying it's between Matt Ryan and the two, Gerlach and Dunn. I'll kill any man who lifts a gun other than them."

"Fair enough." It was a lean, hatchet-faced hand. "This I wanta see."

Lee Dunn sat very still, but he was smiling. "Why, Matt, I reckon mebbe you're right. But you know, Matt, I've heard a sight about you . . . never figured to meet you . . . an' I can't help wonderin', Matt—*are you faster than me?*"

He spoke and he drew and he died falling. He hit dust and he rolled over and he was dead, but he was trying to get up, and then he rolled over again, but he had his gun out. The gun fired and the bullet plowed a furrow and that was all.

Gerlach had not moved. His face was gray and seemed suddenly thinner. As though hypnotized, he stared at the thin tendril of smoke from the muzzle of Ryan's .44 Colt.

Slowly, his tongue touched his dry lips, and he swallowed.

"You boys will be ridin' on," Ryan said quietly. "That rope you got there should be handy. There's a tree down the trail . . . unless you want to ride out with a yella-belly."

"Ain't honin' to," the hatchet-faced man said. He looked down at Lee. "He made his try, Ryan. Give him a send-off, will you?"

Matt nodded, and Kitty walked out and stood beside him, watching them ride away, gathered around Gerlach, who sat his horse as if stunned. Only now his hands were tied.

Matt Ryan looked down at Kitty, and he took her arm and said, "You know, you'll do to ride the river with, Kit. You're a girl to walk beside a man . . . wherever he goes."

"Come in," she said, but her eyes said more than that. "I've some coffee on."

No Man's Mesa

It dominated the desert and the slim green valleys that lay between the peaks or in the canyon bottoms. It was high—over six hundred feet.

The lower part was a talus slope, steep, but it had been climbed. The last three hundred feet was sheer except upon one corner where the rock was shattered and broken edges protruded. This, it was said, was the remnant of the ancient trail to the flat top of the mesa.

There was, legend said, a flowing spring atop the mesa, there were trees and grass and an ancient crater, but all this was talk, for no living man had seen any of it.

The place fostered curious stories. After the Karr boys tried to climb it, there was no rain in the country for two months. After Rison fell from the remnant of the path, there was no rain again. Cattle seemed to shun the place, and people avoided it. The few horses and cattle who did wander to the mesa were soon seen stumbling, vacant-eyed and lonely, losing flesh, growing shaggy of coat, and finally dying. Their whitened bones added to the stories. "This," Old Man Karr often said, "wouldn't be a bad country if it wasn't for Black Mesa."

Matt Calou rode up to Wagonstop in a drenching downpour. When his mount was cared for he sloshed through the rain to the saloon.

"Some storm!" Calou glanced at the four men lining the bar. "Unseasonal, ain't it?"

"Floodin' our gardens." The man jerked his head westward. "It's Black Mesa, that's what it is."

"What's that got to do with it?"

They shrugged. "If you lived in this country you wouldn't have to ask that question."

He took off his slicker and slapped rain from his hat. "Never heard of a pile of rock causin' a rainstorm."

They disdained his ignorance and stared into their drinks. Thunder rumbled, and an occasional lightning flash lit the gloom. Old Man Karr was there, and Wente, who owned the Spring Canyon place. And two hardcase riders from the Pitchfork outfit, Knauf and Russell. Dyer was behind the bar.

Calou was a tall man with a rider's lean build. His face was dark and narrow with an old scar on the cheekbone.

"Lived here long?" he asked Dyer.

"Born here."

"Then you can tell me where the Rafter H lies."

All eyes turned. Dyer stared, then shrugged. "Ain't been a soul on it in fifteen years. Ain't nothin' there but the old stone buildin's and bones. Not even water."

Old Man Karr chuckled. "Right under the edge of Black Mesa, thataway, you couldn't give it to anybody from here. It's cursed, that's what it is."

Matt Calou looked incredulous. "I never put no stock in curses. Anyway, I'm goin' to live there. I bought the Rafter H."

"*Bought* it?" Dyer exploded. "Man, you've been taken. Even if it wasn't near Black Mesa, the place is without water an' overgrown with loco weed."

"What happened? Didn't they used to run cattle there?"

Dyer filled Calou's glass. "Friend," he said quietly, "you'd best learn what you're up against. Twenty-five years ago Art Horan started the Rafter H. Folks warned him about Black Mesa but he laughed. His cattle went loco, his crops died, an' then his well dried up. Finally, he sold out an' left.

"Feller name of Litman took over. Nobody saw him for a few days, an' then a passin' rider found him dead in the yard. Not a mark on him."

"Heart failure, maybe."

"Nobody knows. Litman's nephew came west, but he never liked to stay there at night. Used to spend all his time here, and sometimes he'd camp on the range rather than go near Black Mesa at night.

"Finally, he rounded up a few head of stock, sold 'em, an' drifted. That's one funny part, stranger. Over two thousand head of stock driven to the place, an' never more than five hundred came of it." Dyer nodded his head. "Never seen hide nor hair of 'em."

"Tell him about Horan," Karr suggested. "Tell him that."

"Nobody ever figured that out. After Horan sold out an' then Litman died an' the nephew left, nobody went near the place. One night Wente here, he rode past Black Mesa—"

"I'll never do it again!" Wente stated emphatically. "Never again!"

"He was close to the cliff when he heard a scream, fair make a man's blood run cold, then a crash. He was takin' off when he heard a faint cry, then moanin'. He rode back, an' there on the rocks a man was layin'. He looked up at Wente an' said, 'It got me, too!' an' then he died. The man was Art Horan. Now you figure that out."

"Nobody has lived there since?"

"An' nobody will."

Calou chuckled. "I'll live there. I've got to. Every dime I could beg, borrow, or steal went into that place. I'm movin' in tomorrow."

•　　•　　•

There was animosity in their eyes. The animosity of men who hear their cherished superstitions derided by a stranger. "You think again," Karr replied. "We folks won't allow it. It'll bring bad luck to all of us."

"That's drivel!" Calou replied shortly. "Let me worry about it."

Karr's old face was ugly. "I lost two boys who tried to climb that mesa, an' many a crop lost, an' many a steer because of it. You stay away from there. There's Injun ha'nts atop it, where there was a village once, long ago. They don't like it."

Knauf looked around. "That goes for the Pitchfork, too, mister. Move onto that place an' we'll take steps."

"Such as what?" Calou asked deliberately.

Knauf placed his glass carefully on the bar. "I don't like the way you talk, stranger, an' I reckon it's time you started learnin'."

He was stocky, with thick hands, but when he turned toward Matt Calou there was surprising swiftness in his movements. As he stepped forward he threw a round-house right. Matt Calou was an old hand at this. Catching the swing on his left forearm, he chopped his iron-hand left fist down to Knauf's chin, then followed it with a looping right. Knauf hit the floor and rolled over, gagging.

"Sorry," Calou said. "I wasn't huntin' trouble."

Russell merely stared, then as Calou turned he said, "You'll have the Pitchfork on you now."

"He'll have the whole country on him!" Old Man Karr spat. "Nobody'll sell to you, nobody'll talk to you. If you ain't off this range in one week, you get a coat o' tar an' feathers."

The rain had slackened when Matt Calou rode down into a shallow wash. Water was running knee-high to his horse, but it was not running fast. He crossed and rode through the greasewood of the flat toward the buildings glimpsed in occasional flashes of lightning. Beyond them, dwarfing the country, loomed the towering mass of Black Mesa. When he was still a mile from the house he found the first whitened bones. He counted a dozen skeletons.

Rain pattered on his slicker as he rode into the yard and up to the old stone house. There was a stable, smoke-house, and rock corrals, all built from the talus of the mesa.

Leaving his horse in the stable where it was warm and dry, Matt spilled a bit of grain from a sack behind the saddle into a feed box. "You'll make out on that," he said. "See you in the mornin'."

Rifle under his slicker, he walked to the house. The backdoor lock was rusted, and he braced his foot against the jamb and ripped the lock loose. Once inside, there was a musty smell, but the house floors were solid and the place was in good shape. Opening a window for air, he spread his soogan on the floor and was soon asleep.

It was still raining when he awakened, but washing off the dusty pots and pans, he prepared a hasty break-fast, then saddled up and rode toward the mesa. As he skirted the talus slope he heard water trickling, but when he reached the place where it should have been, there was none. Dismounting, he climbed the slope.

At once he found the stream of runoff. Following it, he found a place where the little stream doubled back and poured into a dark hole at the base of the tower. Listen-ing, he could hear it falling with a roar that seemed to indicate a big, stone-enclosed space. He walked thought-fully back to his horse.

"Well, what did you find?"

Startled at the voice, Matt looked around to see a girl in a rain-darkened gray hat and slicker. Moreover, she had amazingly blue eyes and lovely black hair.

She laughed at his surprise. "I haunt the place," she said, "haven't you heard?"

"They said there were ghosts, but if I'd known they looked like you I'd have been here twice as fast."

She smiled at him. "Oh, I'm not an official ghost! In fact, nobody is even supposed to know I come here, although I suspect a few people do know."

"They've been trying to make the place as unattractive as possible," he said, grinning. "So if they did know, they said nothing."

"I'm Susan Reid. My father has a cabin about five miles from here. He's gathering information on the Indians—their customs, religious beliefs, and folklore."

"And this morning?"

"We saw somebody moving, and Dad's always hoping somebody will climb it so he can get any artifacts there may be up there."

"Any what?"

"Artifacts. Pieces of old pottery, stone tools, or weapons. Anything the Indians might have used."

Together, they rode toward the ranch, talking of the country and of rain. In a few minutes Matt Calou learned more about old Indian pottery than he had imagined anybody could know.

At the crossroads before the Rafter H, they drew up. The rain had ceased, and the sun was struggling to get through. "Matt," she said seriously, "you've started something, so don't underrate the superstition around here. The people who settled here are mostly people from the eastern mountains and they have grown up on such stories. Moreover, some strange things have happened here, and they have some reason for their beliefs. When they talk of running you out, they are serious."

"Then"—he chuckled—"I reckon they'll have to learn the hard way, because I intend to stay right where I am."

When she had gone he went to work. He fixed the lock on the back door, built a door for the stable, and repaired the water trough. He was dead tired when he turned.

At daybreak he was in the saddle checking the boundaries of his land. There was wild land to the north, but he could check on that later. Loco weed had practically taken over some sections of his land, but he knew that animals will rarely touch it if there is ample forage of other grasses and brush. Several of the loco-weed varieties were habit-forming. Scarcity of good forage around water holes or salt grounds was another reason. Most of the poisonous species were early growing and if stock was turned on the range before the grass was sufficiently matured, the cattle would often turn to loco weed.

It was early spring now, but grass was showing in quantity. There was loco weed, but it seemed restricted to a few areas. He had learned in Texas that overgrazing causes the inroad of the weed, but when land is ungrazed the grasses and other growths tend to push the loco back. That had happened here.

The following days found him working dawn until dark. He found some old wire and fenced off the worst sections of weed. Then he borrowed a team from Susan's father and hitched it to a heavy drag made of logs laden with heavy slabs of rock. This drag ripped the weed out by the roots, and once it was loose he raked it into piles for burning.

During all of this time he had seen nobody around. Yet one morning he saddled up, determined to do no work that day. His time was short, as the week they had given him was almost up, and if trouble was coming it might start the following day. He rode north but was turned back by a wall of chaparral growing ten to fifteen feet high, as dense a tangle as he had ever seen in the brush country on the Nueces.

For two miles he skirted the jungle of prickly pear, cat claw, mesquite, and greasewood until he was almost directly behind Black Mesa.

Looking up, he was aware that he was seeing the mesa from an unusual angle. The area was a jumble of upthrust ledges and huge rock slabs and practically impenetrable, yet from where he sat he could see a sort of shadow along the wall of the mesa. Working his way closer, he could see that it was actually an undercut along the face of the cliff. It was visible only because the torrential rains had left the rock damp in the shadow of the cliff. It might be that it had never been seen under these circumstances and from this angle before.

Forcing his horse through a particularly dense mass of brush, he worked a precarious way through the boulders until he was within a few feet of the wall, and near it, of a gigantic earth crack. In the bottom of this crack was a trickle of water, but it was running *toward* the mesa!

Leaving his horse, he descended to the bottom of the crack. At the point where he had left his horse it was all of thirty feet wide, but at the bottom, a man could touch both walls with outstretched arms.

All was deathly still. Only the faint trickle of the water and the crunch of gravel under his boots broke the stillness. Yet he was aware of a distant and subdued roar that seemed to issue from the base of Black Mesa itself!

He came suddenly to a halt. Before him was a vast black hole! Into this trickled the stream he had been following, and far below he could hear the sound of the water falling into a pool. Recalling the small hole on the opposite side, he realized that under Black Mesa lay a huge underground pool or lake. By all reason the water should have been flowing away from the Mesa, but due to the cracks and convulsions of the earth, the water flowed downward into some subterranean basin of volcanic formation.

But if it did not escape? Then there would be a vast reservoir of water, constantly supplied and wholly untapped!

When he emerged, he looked again at the shadow on the wall, revealing a wind- and rain-hollowed undercut that slanted up the side of the mesa. And while he looked he had an idea.

The following day he rode north again, seeking a way through the chaparral. Beyond the belt of brush Sue had told him the green petered out into desert. Although she had not seen it herself, she also told him that only one ranch lay that way, actually to the northwest of Black Mesa, and that was the Pitchfork.

Suddenly he came upon the tracks of two horses. They were shod horses, walking west, and side by side. The tracks ended abruptly as they had begun, at an up-tilted slab of sandstone, but seeing scratches on the sandstone, he rode up himself. It was quite a scramble, but the ledge broke sharply off and a crack, bottomed with blown sand, showed horse tracks.

When he reached the bottom he was in a small meadow and the belt of chaparral was behind him except for scattered clumps. The riders had worked here—he puzzled out the tracks—rounding up a few head of cattle and starting them northwest up the edge of the watery meadow.

Realization flooded over Matt Calou like a cold shower. Wheeling his horse, he started back up the meadow and had gone only a short distance when he came upon a Slash D steer! That was the brand of Dyer, the saloon keeper. Farther along he found another Slash D and three KRs. Grinning with satisfaction, he retracted his steps and rode back to his own ranch.

Sue was in the kitchen and a frying pan was sizzling with bacon and eggs when he returned.

"Eggs!" He grinned at her. "Those are the first eggs I've seen in months!"

"We keep a few chickens," she replied, "and I thought I'd surprise you." She dished up a plate of the eggs and bacon, then poured coffee. "You'd better get ready to leave, young man. Foster, of the Pitchfork, is coming over here with his crowd and the crowd from Wagonstop. They say they'll run you out of the country!"

Calou chuckled. "Let 'em come! I'm ready for 'em now!"

"You look like the cat that swallowed the canary," she said, studying him curiously. "What's happened?"

"Wait an' see!" he teased. "Just wait!"

"You've been working," she said. "What are you going to do with that pasture you dragged?"

"Plant it to crop. After a few years of that I'll let it go back to grass. That will take care of the loco weed."

"Crops take water."

"We'll have lots of water! Plenty of it! Enough for the crops, all the stock, an' baths every night for ourselves and the kids."

She was startled. "Ourselves?"

"My wife and myself."

"You didn't tell me you had a wife!" She stared at him.

"I haven't one, but I sure aim to get one now. I've got one in mind. One that will be the mother of fifteen or twenty kids."

"*Fifteen or twenty?* You're crazy!"

"I like big families. I'm the youngest of twelve boys. Anyway, I got a theory about raisin' 'em. It's like this—"

"It will have to wait," Sue put her hand on his arm. "Here they are."

Matt Calou got to his feet. He was, she realized suddenly, wearing a tied-down gun. His rifle was beside the front door and standing alongside it was a shotgun.

Outside she could see the tall, lean figure of Foster of the Pitchfork and beside him were Russell, Knauf, and a half dozen others. Then, coming up behind them, she saw Old Man Karr, Dyer, and Wente. With them were a dozen riders.

Matt stepped into the door. "Howdy, folks! Glad to

have visitors! I was afraid my neighbors thought I had hydrophobia!"

There were no answering smiles. "We've come to give you a start out of the country, Calou!" Foster said. "We want nobody livin' here!"

Calou smiled, but his eyes were cold as they measured the tall man on the bay horse. "Thoughtful of you, Foster, but I'm stayin', an' if you try to run me off, you'll have some empty saddles, one of which will be a big bay.

"Fact is, I like this place. Once I get a well down, I'll make an easier livin' than you do, Foster."

Something in his tone stiffened Foster and he looked sharply at Matt Calou. Russell moved up beside him and Knauf faded to the left, for a flanking shot.

For a moment there was silence, and Matt Calou laughed, his voice harsh. "Didn't like the sound of that, did you, Foster? I don't reckon your neck feels good inside of hemp, does it? I wonder just what did kill Art Horan, Foster? Was it you? Or did he just get suddenly curious an' come back to find out what happened to all the lost cattle?"

Dyer stared from Calou to Foster, obviously puzzled. "This I don't get," he said. "What's all this talk?"

"Tell him, Foster. You know what I mean."

Foster was trapped. He glanced to right and left, then back to the author of his sudden misery. This was what he had feared if Matt Calou or anyone lived on the Rafter H. His fingers spread on his thigh.

Sue spoke suddenly from a window to the right of the door. "Knauf," she said, "I know why you moved, an' I've got a double-barreled shotgun that will blow you out of your saddle if you lay a hand on your gun!"

"What's goin' on here?" Old Man Karr demanded irritably. "What's he talkin' about, Foss?"

"If he won't tell you"—Matt Calou suddenly stepped

out of the door—"I will. While you folks have been tellin' yourselves ghost stories about Black Mesa, Foster has been bleedin' the range of your cattle."

"You lie!" Foster roared. "You lie like—!" He grabbed for his gun and Matt Calou fired twice. The first shot knocked the gun from Foster's suddenly bloody hand, and the second notched his ear. It was a bullet that would have killed Foster had he not flinched from the hand wound.

Russell's face was pale as death and he gripped the pommel hard with both hands.

Dyer's face was stern. "All right, Calou! You clear this up an' fast or there'll be a necktie party right here, gun or no gun."

"Your cattle," Matt explained coolly, "hunted water an' found it where nobody knew there was any. Then Foster found your cattle. Ever since then he's been sweepin' that draw ever' few days, takin' up all the cattle he found there, regardless of brand. You lost cattle, but you saw no marks of rustlin', no tracks, no reason to suspect anybody. An' you were all too busy blamin' Black Mesa for all your troubles. Your cattle drifted that way an' never came back, an' Foster was gettin' rich. All he had to do was ride down that draw back of Black Mesa, just beyond the chaparral.

"As for Black Mesa, the reason you thought you saw something movin' up there was because you did see something. The cows that they originally had on the Rafter H are up there, I imagine."

"That ain't possible!" Old Man Karr objected. "Not even a man could climb that tower!"

"There's a crack on the other side, an undercut that makes a fairly easy trail up. Cattle have been grazin' up there for years, an' there's several square miles of good graze up there."

Foster got clumsily from the saddle and commenced to struggle with his hand. One of the men got down to help him. Old Man Karr chewed angrily at his mustache,

---

half resenting the exploded fears of the mountain. Dyer hesitated, then looked down at Matt. "Guess we been a passel o' fools, stranger," he said. "The drinks are on us."

Dyer looked down at Foster. "But I reckon it's a good thing we brought along a rope."

Foster paled under his deep tan. "Give me a break, Dyer!" he pleaded. "I'll pay off! I got records! Sure, I done it, an' I was a fool, but it was an awful temptation. I was broke when I started, an' then—"

"We'll have an accounting," Wente said stiffly, "then we'll decide. If you can take care of our losses, we might make a deal."

Together, Matt and Sue watched them walk away. "If you didn't want fifteen or twenty children," she suggested tentatively, "I know a girl who might be interested."

Matt grinned. "How about six?"

"I guess that's not too many."

He slipped his arm around her waist. "Then consider your proposal accepted."

Sunlight bathed the rim of Black Mesa with a sudden halo. A wide-eyed range cow lowed softly to her calf, unaware of mystery. The calf stumbled to its feet, brushing a white, curved fragment, fragile as a leaf.

It was the weathered lip of an ancient baked clay jar.

GILA CROSSING

I

There was an old wooden trough in front of the livery barn in Gila Crossing and at one end of the trough a rusty pump. When Jim Sartain rode up the dusty street, four men, unshaven and tired, stood in a knot by the pump, their faces somber with dejection.

Two of the men were tall, but in striking contrast otherwise. Ad Loring was a Pennsylvania man, white-haired but with a face rough-hewn and strong. It was a thoughtful face, but resolute as well. The man beside him was equally tall but much heavier, sullen and black-browed, with surly, contemptuous eyes. His jaw was a chunk of granite above the muscular column of his neck. Roy Strider was the kind of man he looked, domineering and quick to use his muscular strength.

Peabody and McNabb were equally contrasting. McNabb, as dry and dour as his name suggested, with narrow gray eyes and the expression of a man hard-driven but far from beaten. Peabody carried a shotgun in the hollow of his arm. He was short, and inclined to stoutness. Like the others, he turned to look at the man on the dusty roan when he dismounted and walked to the pump. The roan moved to the trough and sank his muzzle gratefully into the cool water.

Sartain was conscious of their stares, yet he gave no

sign. Taking down the gourd dipper, he shook out the few remaining drops and began to pump the protesting handle.

The men studied his dusty gray shirt as if to read his mission from the breadth of his powerful shoulders. Their eyes fell to the walnut-butted guns, long-hung and tied down, to the polished boots now dust-covered, and the Mexican-type spurs. Jim Sartain drank deep of the cold water, a few drops falling down his chin and shirtfront. He emptied two dippers before he stopped drinking.

Even as he drank, his mind was cataloging these men, their dress, their manner, and their weapons. He was also studying the fat man who sat in the huge chair against the wall of the barn, a man unshaven and untidy, with a huge face, flabby lips, and the big eyes of a hungry hound.

This fat man heaved himself from his chair. "Put up your hoss, stranger? I'm the liveryman." His shirt bulged open in front and the rawhide thong that served as a belt held his stomach in and his pants up. "Name of George Noll." He added, "Folks around here know me."

"Put him in a stall and give him a bait of grain," Sartain said. "I like him well fed. And be careful, he's touchy."

Noll chuckled flatly. "Them hammerheads are all ornery." His eyes, sad, curious, rolled to Sartain. "Goin' fer? Or are you here?"

"I'm here." Sartain's dark eyes were as unreadable as his face. "Seems to have been some fire around. All the range for miles is burned off." The men beside him would have suffered from that fire. They would be from the wagons behind the firebreak in the creek bottom. "Noticed a firebreak back yonder. Somebody did some fast work to get that done in time."

"That was Loring here," Noll offered. "Had most of it done before the fire. He figured it was coming."

Sartain glanced at Loring. "You were warned? Or was it an accident?"

But it was Strider who spoke. "Accident!" The dark-browed man spat the word. Then he stared at Sartain, his eyes sullen with suspicion. "You ask a lot of questions for a stranger."

Sartain turned his black eyes to Strider and looked at him steadily while the seconds passed, a look that brought dark blood to Strider's face and a hard set to the brutal jaw. "That's right," Sartain said at last. "When I want to know something I figure that's the way to find it out." His eyes swung back to Loring, ignoring Strider.

"We assume we were burned out by the big ranchers," Loring replied carefully. "We've been warned to leave, but we shall continue to stay. We are not men to be driven from our homes, and the land is open to settlement.

"Three ranchers control approximately a hundred miles of range. Stephen Bayne, Holston Walker, and Colonel Avery Quarterman. We deliberately chose a location that would interfere as little as possible, moving into the mountainous foothills of Black Mesa, north of the Middle Fork. Despite that, there was trouble."

"With the men you named?"

"Who else? Bayne accused Peabody of butchering a B Bar steer, and at Peabody's denial there would have been shooting except that McNabb and I were both there. Then a few days ago Peabody and I rode to Oren McNabb's place, the brother to this gentleman, and found him dead. He had been shot down while unarmed. His stock had been run off, his buildings burned."

"Then there was a rumpus here at the Crossin'," Peabody said. "Loring, Strider, an' me, we jumped Colonel Quarterman on the street. He was mighty stiff, said he knew of no murder and we could get out or take the consequences. Strider here, he came right out an' accused him of murder, then called him out."

"He didn't fight?"

"He's yeller!" Strider sneered. "Yeller as saffron! With no riders at his back he'd never raise a hand to no man!"

"Sometimes," Sartain replied dryly, "it needs more courage to avoid a fight. If this Quarterman is the one I've heard of, he has proved his courage more than once. He's a salty old Injun fighter."

"So he kills a lone rancher who's unarmed?" Again Strider sneered. The big man's dislike for Jim Sartain was evident.

"Had you thought somebody else might have done it? Did you find him there? Or any evidence of him or his riders?"

"Who else would have done it? Or could have done it?"

"You might have."

"*Me?*" Strider jerked as if struck and his face went pale, then ugly with fury.

"Hold your hand, Roy." George Noll was speaking from the barn door, and there was unexpected authority in his tone, casual as it sounded. "Draw on this hombre an' you'll die. He's the Ranger, Jim Sartain."

II

Strider's big hand was spread above his gun butt and it froze there, then slowly eased to his side. "Sorry," he said resentfully. "I didn't know you was no Ranger."

It was not respect for the law that stopped Strider. Nor was it fear; blustering he might be, but not afraid.

"I was saying that you might have done it," Sartain repeated, "or Loring, or myself. You have no more evidence against the ranchers than they would have against us."

"That's what I've said, Roy," Loring interposed. "We can't go off half-cocked when it will lead to bloodshed. The odds are all against us, anyway. Before we move we must be sure."

"This Ranger won't help *us* any!" Peabody declared. "Who sent for you . . . Quarterman?"

"That's right, and that should prove something to you. If he were guilty he wouldn't call in a Ranger, he'd wipe you out himself, and they must muster a hundred riders between them. He thinks there is something else behind this."

"He does, does he?" Strider sneered. "All he called you for was to get it done legal."

Noll walked up on the other side of the trough. "Hotel up the street. Clean beds, too, an' down thisaway a mite Amy Booth has her eatin' house. Best grub west o' the Pecos. Reckon I'll see you there."

Sartain nodded, then turned back to Loring. "You men take it easy. I'll look into this."

"An' we starve while you do?" McNabb spoke for the first time, bitterness edging his voice. "Man, those wagons you saw belong to us! Those women an' kids are ours! We're nigh out of grub an' our stock's been run off! How can we wait? What can we do? You talk about takin' it easy! Them ain't *your* womenfolks!"

"Will it help if you crowd those cowhands into a gunfight an' get killed? How would your families leave the country then? Who would care for them? Be patient, man!"

They were silent, acknowledgment of the truth of what he had said obvious on their faces. Grim, lonely, frightened men. Not frightened of trouble for themselves, for they had known thirst, dust storms, and flash floods, they had fought Indians and hunger. They were frightened of an uncertain future and what would become of their families. "We'll sit tight," Loring said. "I never heard of you giving a man a raw deal yet!"

At that moment the three ranchers awaited him at the Longhorn Hotel up the street, and Sartain knew their appearance now would have led to shooting. Furthermore, their riders would be in town tonight, so the situation was like a powder keg.

The quiet authority he remembered in Noll's voice made him wonder, it was so unexpected. The man seemed to have judgment and might provide the essential balance wheel the community needed.

Quarterman was a tall man of nearly sixty with a white mustache and goatee. He stood up when Sartain entered, an immaculate man in a black broadcloth coat and white hat. His blue eyes twinkled as he held out his hand. Beside him was a tall girl with dark eyes and hair, her figure lovely. She looked at him, then again. "How are you, Colonel? I'm Sartain."

"Recognized you, sir, from stories I've heard. Mr. Sartain, my daughter, Carol." He turned slightly toward a big young man with red hair and a rugged face. "This is Steve Bayne, and the other gentleman"—he indicated a short, powerful man with a broad-jawed face and keen blue eyes—"is Holston Walker, of the Running W."

Jim Sartain acknowledged the introductions, aware of the possessive air adopted by Bayne toward Carol, and to his wry amusement, he found himself resenting it.

It was Walker who interested him most. Holy Walker was a successful rancher, but stories of his skill with his deadly six-guns were told wherever cowhands congregated, and also of his almost fabulous treatment of his hands.

As their hands gripped, Sartain thought he had never felt such power latent in any man as in the leonine Walker. His rusty hair showed no hint of gray, and his face was smooth, the skin taut over the powerful bones of his face.

"There's been a lot of range burned off," Sartain commented. "Who did that?"

"The nesters," Bayne said irritably. "Who else would do it?"

"They claim some of you did it," Sartain suggested mildly. "Maybe you're both wrong."

Bayne stared at him. "Who did you come here to act for?" he demanded. "Those infernal nesters or us?"

"For neither of you," Sartain replied. "I'm to see justice done, to find who is breaking the law and see they are punished, whoever they may be. The law," he added, "is not an instrument to protect any certain group against another."

Bayne turned on Quarterman. "I told you it wouldn't do any good to send for Rangers, Colonel! We could handle this better our own way! Let me turn John Pole loose on them! He'll have them out of here, and mighty fast!"

"Let me hear of you starting anything like that," Sartain said coolly, "and you'll be thrown in jail."

Bayne turned on him impatiently. "You fatheaded fool! Who do you think you are? I've fifty riders at my call, and a dozen of them better men than you! We don't need any overrated, blown-up Ranger braggarts to do our fighting!"

Sartain smiled. It was a rare smile and had a warm, friendly quality. He glanced at Quarterman, and then his daughter. "Evidently opinions are divided," he said dryly. He turned back to Bayne. "I'm not here to resent your opinions of the Texas Rangers"—there was no smile in his eyes now—"I'm here to settle your trouble, and I will settle it. However," he added, "if you have any more riders of the quality of John Pole, it's no wonder you've got trouble. He's a known killer, and a suspected rustler. He's been a troublemaker everywhere he's gone. It might go far toward solving the situation if he were fired and packed out of the country."

Bayne snorted his contempt. "Riders like Pole helped build my ranch," he said. "I want men in my outfit who can handle guns, and as for his being a killer, at least he hasn't been hiding behind the skirts of the law!"

"Here, here, Steve!" Quarterman interrupted. "That's no way to talk! Sartain is here at my request, and we aren't getting any results this way!"

"By the way, Colonel"—Sartain turned toward Quarterman—"I want to get about six head of beef to feed those people in the creek bottom. We can't let them starve."

Stephen Bayne had started to walk away, now he whirled and charged back, eyes bulging. *"What?"* he roared. "You ask us to feed those lousy beggars? Why, you—"

Jim Sartain's face was suddenly hard and cold. "You've said enough, Bayne! I'll let you get away with it because I'm here on business! You finish that statement and I'll slap all your teeth down your throat!"

Devilish eagerness sprang into Bayne's face. "Stinkin' coward, was what I was goin' to call you," he said deliberately.

III

Sartain's hands were chest-high in front of him as he was rubbing the fingers of his right hand against the palm of his left. Now, at Bayne's words, his left leaped like a striking rattler and his hard knuckles smashed Bayne's lips back into his teeth. The blow stopped Bayne in his tracks momentarily, and that was all Sartain wanted. He moved in fast with all his bottled-up anger exploding in smashing punches.

A left and right to the wind that jerked Bayne's mouth wide as he gasped for his lost wind, and then a cracking right to the jaw that felled him to his knees, his face contorted with fury and pain.

Sartain was cool. He glanced quickly at Quarterman, who was obviously astonished, and at Holy Walker, who smiled faintly. "You move fast, friend," he said quietly.

Then his eyes went to Carol, who was staring down at Steve Bayne, a peculiar expression on her face, then she looked up at Jim Sartain. "I'm sorry, Miss Quarterman," he said. "He asked for it. I wasn't looking for trouble."

"You accept your opportunities quickly, though, don't you?" she asked coldly. "No wonder you've killed men."

"Nobody would have been surprised had I drawn. Men have been killed for less," he replied. He turned back to Quarterman. "I want to renew my request, Colonel. I appreciate the situation, but your fight is not with women and children, and these are good, honest people. How about it?"

Quarterman hesitated, gnawing his mustache, resenting the position he was in. Behind Sartain, Walker spoke. "I reckon I can spare a few head, but those are proud folks. Will they take them?"

Sartain turned. "Thanks, Walker. An' let's go see, shall we?"

"May I come along?"

Sartain turned on Carol, surprised and pleased. "Glad to have you, ma'am. We sure are!"

Fires blazed cheerfully among the huddle of wagons. There were ten families there, and seventeen children in all. As the three rode toward the fires a man stepped from the shadows with a shotgun. It was Peabody.

"What you want?" he demanded suspiciously, glancing from Sartain to Holy Walker. Then he detected Carol Quarterman and he jerked his hat off in confusion. "Pardon me, ma'am." His eyes went back to the men. "What is this, Ranger? What you want?"

"A talk with you, Loring, and McNabb. Right here will do."

"I reckon not." McNabb stepped from the shadows near a wagon with a Spencer over his arm. "Anything to be said will be said to all of us, right in the circle!"

Dismounting, they followed McNabb into the firelight. Loring got to his feet, and beside him, Strider. A buxom woman with a face crimson from the fire turned and looked up at them, and a young woman holding a very young baby moved closer, her eyes grave and frightened.

Surprisingly, Walker took the initiative. "You folks know who I am, but I don't think we've been very neighborly. Now I know what it means to lose an outfit because I lost mine a couple of times. If I can help any, I'd be right glad to."

McNabb's voice was brittle. "We ain't askin' nor takin' any help from you! We ain't on charity!"

Strider thrust forward. "This here's a trick!" he exploded. "I don't like the look of it! Why should you give us anythin'? So's you can find the hides in our camp later, after you kill us? Look mighty bad for us, wouldn't it?"

"Don't be a fool, man!" Walker replied impatiently. "We didn't want you people here, but you've come an' stayed. You never bothered me, but you did take water we needed. That's not the question now. You've been burned out, an' we're neighbors."

"So you want to help?" Strider sneered. "Well, we don't need your help!"

"Walker volunteered, Strider," Sartain interposed. "I told Quarterman the situation and Walker offered to help."

"We don't need no help! Why didn't he think of that before he burned us out?"

"I didn't burn you out!" Walker declared irritably. "I—"

"You didn't burn us out?" A wiry little man with a face like a terrier thrust himself forward, his eyes burning. "You're a dir—!"

Loring grabbed the man by the arm and flung him bodily back into the darkness. "Grab that man, somebody!" Loring shouted. "What's the matter? You men gone crazy? Do you want to start a gunfight here among our women and children?"

For once Sartain was stopped. The deep antagonisms here were beyond reason, and Walker, although a generous man, was also an impatient one. He would take little more of this. Then into the gap where anything might have happened stepped Carol Quarterman. She went directly to the woman with the baby in her arms. She was smiling with genuine interest, and holding out her arms to the child. "Oh, look at him! Isn't he a darling? And his hair . . . it's so red!"

The girl flushed with pleasure, and the baby responded simply and stretched out his little arms to Carol. She took him, then looked at the girl, smiling. "What's his name? How old is he?"

"He's ten months," the girl said, wiping her palms on her apron, "his name's Earl . . . after my husband." A tall, shy young man with big hands and a shock of blond, curly hair grinned at Carol.

"He's big for his age," he volunteered. "I reckon he'll be quite a man."

Sartain looked at Carol with genuine respect. In the moment when the situation seemed rapidly slipping out of control she had stepped neatly into the breach and in one instant had established a bond of warmth and sympathy. Strider stared at the girls and the child, and Holy Walker's face relaxed.

"How about the beef?" Sartain asked Loring.

"Not for me!" McNabb was stiff-necked and angry. "I won't take charity!"

The woman bending over the fire straightened up, holding a ladle in her hand which she pointed at the man. "Angus McNabb! I'm surprised at you! Talkin' of charity! These are good folks an' it's right neighborly of them to offer it! Have you forgotten the time Lew Fuller's house burned down back on the Washita? We all got together an' helped them! It ain't charity, just bein' neighborly!"

The blond-headed Earl looked around. "You send one of your hands with me, Mr. Walker," he said, "an' I'll ride for that beef, an' thank you a mighty lot."

"Then it's settled!" Walker said. "Maybe if we folks had got together before we'd not have had this trouble."

IV

Jim Sartain built a smoke and looked thoughtfully at the men. For the moment the issue was sidetracked, yet nothing was settled. Underneath, the problem remained, and the bitter antagonisms. McNabb was bitter, and Roy Strider belligerent, and he knew that Steve Bayne would be likewise. The real sore spot was still to be uncovered.

Back at the livery barn George Noll had watched the three ride by, and there had been no gunfire from the bottom. He bit off a corner of his plug tobacco, and watched Steve Bayne draw nearer. An instant his jaws ceased to move, then began again, a methodical chewing.

"Howdy!" He jerked his head toward the bottom. "Looks like that Ranger an' Holy Walker fixed things up. First thing you know they'll be back in the canyons livin' off beef."

"Not mine, they won't!" Bayne turned his angry eyes on Noll. "Holy may soften up for that Ranger's talk, but not me! The Colonel was a fool to send for him! We can handle our own affairs!"

"That's what I always say," Noll agreed. "Well, that fire was a godsend, anyway. It got them off the range. If they are smart they'll keep movin' . . . fact is," he suggested, rolling his tobacco in his cheeks, "they oughta be kept movin'."

Bayne scowled. Success had made him bigheaded, and he was unable to distinguish between luck and ability. He had had luck, but more than that, he owed much of his success to John Pole's running iron. More of it than to his own handling of cattle.

Colonel Avery Quarterman, he had decided, was an old fool. He said nothing because he wanted to marry Carol. Holy Walker he resented, partly for his reputation, and partly because there was no escaping the fact that Walker's was a tightly managed outfit, and a very profitable one. Bayne had the feeling that Walker despised him.

He was positive now that they were taking the wrong tack. He was confident that the nesters would not fight, but would run at the first show of force. Nothing in his experience fitted him to judge men like McNabb, Peabody, or Loring. Bayne had respect for obvious strength and contempt for all else, a contempt grown from ignorance.

Had anyone suggested that his feelings had been carefully nurtured by George Noll, he would have been furious. Noll had found many men open to suggestion, but the two he handled most easily were Strider and Bayne.

Seated unshaven against the wall of his barn, his sockless feet in broken shoes, his shirt collar always greasy with dirt, his gray hat showing finger marks, he was not a man to inspire respect or confidence, yet the barn was a focal point, and he heard much and was able to drop his own seemingly casual remarks.

He was a cunning man, and he possessed the power to hate beyond that of most men. His hatred had been a rambling and occasional thing until that day in the livery barn when he made advances to Carol Quarterman.

He had mistaken her friendly air for invitation, and one day when stabling her mare, he put his hands on her. She sprang away with such loathing and contempt that it bit much deeper than the lash of her quirt across his face, and something black and ugly burst within him. He sprang for her, and only the arrival of Holy Walker had saved her. Walker had come quickly into the barn, but had seen nothing.

Not wanting her father to kill Noll, Carol said nothing, but took care to avoid him. Yet George Noll's anger burned deep and brooding, and he began to plot and plan. If Quarterman were destroyed, and the girl in need, he would see her pride humbled. Had it required much effort, the chances were that he would have done nothing, but the situation was sparking, and needed only someone to fan the blaze.

He chewed tobacco in silence while the insult to his pride grew enormously. As all ignorant men, he possessed great vanity, and nothing had prepared him for the loathing on the face of Carol Quarterman. His lewd eyes watched her coming and going, and her bright laughter seemed to be mocking him. He could not believe she had almost forgotten his action, and believed she deliberately tormented him.

Carefully, he fed the flames of envy and resentment in Roy Strider, and the vanity and contempt of Steve Bayne. It was only a step to outright trouble, which began when Roy Strider gave a beating to a Bar B cowhand in a fistfight. Bayne was furious and would have ridden down on Strider at once but for Quarterman.

Noll, who knew most things, knew that John Pole was rustling, but hinted to Quarterman and Walker that it was the nesters. All he actually said was a remark that they always had beef, but such an idea grows and feeds upon uncertainty and suspicion.

His hints to Bayne had apparently sown the seeds of action, for he saw the young rancher stride purposefully down the street to join in a long conversation with John Pole, Nelson, and Fowler. Pole, a lean, saturnine man, seemed pleased. Noll spat and chuckled to himself.

Sartain walked up the street, his boot heels sounding loud upon the boardwalk, and Carol Quarterman, watching him draw near, felt a curious little throb of excitement.

How tall he was! And the way he walked, it was more the quick, lithe step of a woodsman—speaking of strong, well-trained muscles—than the walk of any rider. Yet she sensed worry in him now. "What's the matter, Ranger?" she asked, smiling. "Troubles? I thought we settled things."

"We've settled nothing." His voice was worried. "You know that. There is a bit of kindly feeling now, but how long will it last? The basic trouble is still there, and what is it? Where is it? Who can gain by trouble?"

She caught something of his mood. "I see what you mean. It is strange how such things start. Father and Holy griped a little when they moved in, but only Steve seemed much impressed by it, and he is always being impressed by something. Then cattle were missed and we warned them off. They wouldn't go."

He nodded. "I've seen these things start before, but always with much more reason. It's almost as if somebody *wanted* trouble. I've seen that, too, but who could profit from it here?"

"Nobody ever seems to win in a fight," Carol agreed. "Everyone gets hurt. The only way anyone could hope to win would be to stay out of it and pick up the pieces."

Sartain nodded, musing. "There are other motives. Men have been known to do ugly things without any hope of gain, over a woman, or out of envy or jealousy. There seems no way to realize any gain, but unless there is somebody around who hates either the ranchers or the nesters, I can't figure it."

"There's nobody I know of," she said doubtfully. It was odd that right then she remembered George Noll, but it was absurd to think all this could stem from so small a thing.

"Steve is angry enough to kill you," Carol said suddenly. "He'll get over it, but the fact that you knocked him down hurt worse than the blows."

She was realizing then that her feelings toward Steve had undergone a change. For months she had been resigned to the idea of marriage to him. He was handsome, and could be very charming, yet she had never been in love with him, and now in comparison with Sartain he seemed suddenly very juvenile, with his easy angers, his vanity and petulance. "Be careful," she warned Sartain. "Steve might go further than we believe. He's very sure of his rightness."

"In a way," he replied, "I can understand his not liking me. He's in love with you and he can see very well that I like you!"

The suddenness of it took her breath, but before she could make any reply, he stepped from the walk and strode quickly away. Yet as he was walking off, incongruously, a remark of Carol's recurred to him. *The only way to win,* she had said, *would be to stay out of it and pick up the pieces.*

Yet if the cattlemen and nesters fought, who would be left to pick up any pieces? He spent a busy afternoon and evening, visiting the town's banker, the doctor, both of the lawyers, and two keepers of stores. When he left the last one he was very thoughtful. He had learned a little, but it was all very flimsy, too flimsy.

V

Surprisingly, the night passed quietly. When it was well past midnight Sartain returned to the hotel and to bed. He awakened with the sun streaming through his window and the street full of excited shouts. Hurriedly scrambling into his clothes, he rushed for the street.

Men were crowding the street, most of them riders from the ranches, and Steve Bayne was up on the steps of the harness shop shouting at them, his face red and angry. Sartain broke through the crowd and confronted him. "What's going on here?" he demanded.

Bayne wheeled on him, his eyes ugly. "You!" He

sneered. "You and your peacemaking! The damn nester killed Parrish!"

"What nester?" he asked patiently. "Who's Parrish?"

"Parrish"—Bayne's face was flushed with temper— "was Holy Walker's cowhand who went after those cattle with Earl Mason. Mason killed him!"

"That doesn't make sense," Sartain replied calmly. "You are telling us Mason killed a man who was getting beef for him?" He spoke loudly so the assembled crowd could hear.

"What you think doesn't matter!" Bayne bellowed. "Parrish was found dead along the trail, *an' we're hangin' Mason right now!*"

A half-dozen rough-handed men were shoving Mason forward, their faces dark with passion. Another man had a rope.

Suddenly someone shouted, "Look out! Here come the nesters!"

They were coming, all right, a tight little band of hardheaded, frightened men. Frightened, but ready to fight for what they believed.

Sartain wheeled. "Quarterman! Walker! Call off your men! Send them back to the ranches and tell them to stay there! If one shot is fired in this street by those men, I'll hold you accountable!"

"It's too far gone to stop now," Quarterman said. "Mason killed Parrish, all right."

"Call them off!" Sartain warned. "Get them off this street at once or you'll be held accountable! There's going to be blazing hell if you don't!"

Bayne laughed. "Why, you meddling fool! You can't stop this now! Nothing can stop it! Pole, the second those nesters pass that water trough, cut them down!"

Time for talking was past, and Sartain struck swiftly. Steve Bayne never even got his hands up. Sartain struck left and right so fast the rancher had no chance even to partially block the punches. Both caught him in the wind, yet even as he gasped for breath Jim Sartain grabbed him around the waist, spun him around, and jammed a six-gun into his spine. "Pole!" he yelled. "One shot and I'll kill Bayne! I'll shoot him right here, and you'll be next! Get off the street!"

He shoved Bayne forward. "Tell them!" he snapped. "Order them off the street or I'll blow you apart!"

Bayne gasped the words: "I will not!"

Sartain groaned inwardly. The nesters were almost to the trough, and although outnumbered at least five to one, they kept coming. His pistol barrel came up and he slapped Bayne across the skull with it, one sweeping blow that dropped him to the dust.

Springing over him, his face dark with bitter fury, he faced the mob, both guns drawn now. "All right!" His voice roared in the suddenly silent street. "You wanted a fight! By the Lord Harry, you can have it and now! *With me!*

"Back up! Get off the street or start shootin' an' I'll kill the first man who lifts a gun! I've got twelve shots here and I never miss! Who wants to die?"

His eyes bazing, trembling with fury, he started for the mob. It was a colossal bluff, and one from which he could not turn back, yet stop that slaughter he would, if he must die to do it.

"Back up!" His fury was mounting now and the mob seemed half-hypnotized by it. Not a man in that crowd but knew the reputation of Jim Sartain and the unerring marksmanship of which those guns were capable. They recalled that he had at one time shot it out with five men and come out unscathed. To each the black muzzles of the guns seemed pointed directly at himself, and not a man of them but suddenly believed that he had but to lift a hand to die.

Behind him the nesters were equally appalled. A lone man had sprung between them and almost certain death, and that man was slowly but surely backing the crowd up the street.

Carol Quarterman, her heart pounding, watched from the door of the hotel. At first, one man shifted his feet, but the feeling of movement caught the mob and those in front, eager to be out of reach of those guns, felt their backing easing away from them, and they, too, backed away, almost without conscious thought.

Then Sartain called out. "Quarterman! Walker! You get a last chance! Order these men back to their ranches or I'll see you both jailed for inciting to riot! If a man dies here today I'll see you both hang for murder!"

VI

Quarterman stiffened. "You needn't warn me, Sartain. I know my duty." He lifted his voice. "Mount up, men, and go home. We'll let the law handle this."

Walker added his voice, and the cowhands, aware of a cool breath of relief, were suddenly finding the street too narrow for comfort.

Sartain turned to see the rope on Mason's neck, and John Pole standing beside him, and only a few feet away, Newton and Fowler. "Take off that rope, Pole!" he said sharply.

The gunman's face was cold. "I'll be damned if I do!" he flared.

Sartain was suddenly quiet inside. "Take it off," he repeated, "and with mighty easy hands!"

Carefully, John Pole let go the rope. He stepped a full step to one side, his arms bent at the elbows, hands hovering above his guns. "You threw a mighty big bluff, Ranger," he said, "but I'm callin' it!"

Carol Quarterman saw Pole's hands move, and as if all feeling and emotion were suddenly arrested, she saw Sartain's hands move at the same instant. And then she saw the lifting muzzle of a rifle from the livery-stable door!

"*Jim!*" Her cry was agonized. "Look out! *The stable!*"

Sartain, his eyes blazing from beneath the brim of his low-crowned hat, palmed his guns and fired. It was that flashing, incredible draw, yet even as his right gun spat flame he heard Carol's cry.

A thundering report blasted on his right and he was knocked sprawling, his right-hand gun flying from him. Throwing his left gun over, he caught it deftly with his right hand and snapped a quick shot at the black interior of the barn, just below the round muzzle of a Spencer.

His head was reeling and the street seemed to be rocking and tipping, yet he got his feet under him.

John Pole was still erect, but his blue shirt was stained with blood and his guns were flowering with dancing blooms of flame. Guns seemed to be thundering everywhere and he started forward, firing again.

Staggering, Sartain lurched toward Pole and saw a shot kick up dust beyond the gunman, and believed he'd missed, having no realization that the shot had kicked dust only after passing through him.

Amazed, he saw Pole was on the ground, clawing at the dirt with bloody hands. A gun bellowed again from the barn door and he turned, falling to his face in the dust. He could taste blood in his mouth and his head felt big as a balloon, but he struggled to his feet, thumbing shells into his gun. Again a shot blasted from the barn, but he kept walking, then caught the side of the door with his left hand and peered into the gloom.

George Noll, his flabby face gray, stared at him with bulging, horror-filled eyes. He had a rifle in his hands and he stared from it to Sartain with amazement. And then Jim lifted his six-gun level and fired three fast shots.

Noll caught them in his bulging stomach and he went up on his toes, mumbled some words lost in the froth of blood at his lips, then pitched over to grind his face into the hay and dirt of the floor.

Sartain's knees seemed suddenly to vanish and the floor struck him in the mouth, and the last thing he remembered was the taste of dirt and straw in his mouth, and the sound of running feet. . . .

For a long time he was aware of nothing, and then there was sunlight through a window, a pump complaining, and a woman's voice singing. He was lying now in a strange bed, and the hand that lay on the coverlet was much whiter than when he had last seen it.

A door opened and he looked into the eyes of Carol Quarterman. "Well!" she exclaimed. "I didn't think you were ever coming out of it! How do you feel?"

"I . . . don't really know. What house is this?"

"Dr. Hassett's. He's my uncle and your doctor. I'm your nurse, and you had four bullets in you, two rifle, and two pistol. That's what Uncle Ed says, although I don't think he could tell one from the other."

"Noll?"

"He's dead. You grazed him once, hit him three times. John Pole is dead, too. You . . . killed him."

"Wasn't there some other shooting?"

"That was Holy Walker and Dad. They finished off Newton and Fowler when they started to help Pole. Dad got hit in the side, but not badly, but Walker wasn't scratched."

"Mason?"

"He was luckiest of all. He was hit three times by bullets aimed at other people and none of them more than broke the skin. All of them are back in the canyons again, and not even Steve Bayne has a word to say."

"How long have I been here?"

"A week, and you'd better settle down for a long rest. Uncle Ed says you can't be moved and that you'll have to stay in bed, with me to nurse you, for at least two more weeks."

Sartain grinned. "With you as nurse? I'll go for that, but what about Steve Bayne?"

She shrugged. "He's gone back to his ranch with more headaches than the one you gave him. Pole had been rustling, branding some of it with Steve's Bar B and selling the rest. Newton worked with him, and he talked before he died; he also swore he saw George Noll set the fire on the range that burned everybody out.

"Apparently he hated me, but when they went through his office they found figures showing how he had planned to buy up the ranches after the range war killed off most of the men. The questions you asked around town started the investigation of his effects, and proved you'd guessed right. As you knew, he was the only one with money enough to take advantage of the situation the range war would leave."

"Anything on Parrish?"

"Nothing exact. However, he had been back to the ranch and talked with the wrangler after leaving Mason. Probably that was Pole. Parrish must have caught him rustling, but we'll never know."

Jim Sartain stared out of the window at the sunlit street. He could see the water trough and the two lone trees. A man sat on the edge of the walk, whittling in the sun. A child was chasing a ball. Farther along, a gray horse stamped a patient foot and flicked casually at the flies.

It was a quiet street, a peaceful street. Someday all the West would be like Gila Crossing. . . .

MEDICINE GROUND

A Cactus Kid Story

The Cactus Kid was in a benevolent mood and the recent demise of Señor "Ace" Fernandez was far from his thoughts. Had the Kid's own guns blasted a trail down the slippery ladder to Hell, he would have been wary, for he knew well the temper of the four brothers Fernandez.

He had not, however, done a personal gun job on Ace. He had merely acted for the moment as the finger of destiny, and but for a certain small action of his, the agile fingers of the elder Fernandez might still be fleecing all and sundry at the Cantina.

Nobody who knew him could question the Kid's sense of humor, and it extended as far as poker, which is very far indeed. The humor of Martin Jim (so-called because he was the second of two Jim Martins to arrive in Aragon) was another story. Jim had a sense of humor all right, but it ended somewhere south of poker. Martin Jim was a big, muscular man who packed a pistol for use.

On the memorable afternoon of Ace's death, that gentleman was sitting in a little game with Martin Jim, the Cactus Kid, Pat Gruen, and an itinerant miner known as Rawhide. The Kid, being the observant type, had taken note of the smooth efficiency of Señor Ace when he handled the cards. He also noted the results of a couple of subsequent hands. Thereafter the Kid was careful to drop out when Ace was doing the dealing. The others, being less knowing and more trustful, stayed in the game, and as a result the pile of poker chips in front of Ace Fernandez had grown to an immodest proportion.

Finally, when Pat Gruen and Rawhide were about broke, there came a hand from which all dropped away but Ace Fernandez and Martin Jim. With twelve hundred dollars of his hard-earned money (cowhands were making forty a month!) in the center of the table, Martin Jim's sense of humor had reached the vanishing point.

The Cactus Kid, idly watching the game, had seen the black sheep lead the burly lamb to the slaughter; he also chanced to glimpse the cards Ace Fernandez turned up. He held a pair of fours, a nine, ten, and a queen. A few minutes later his eyes shifted back to the hand Fernandez held and there was no nine, ten, or queen, but three aces were cuddling close to the original pair of fours.

Naturally, this phenomenon interested him no end, especially so as he had seen the way, an odd way, too, Ace held his arm.

When the showdown came, Martin Jim laid down two pair, and Ace Fernandez, looking very smug, his full house.

Leaning forward as if to see the cards better, the Cactus Kid deftly pushed the cuff of Ace's white sleeve over the head of a nail that projected an inch or so from the edge of the table.

Smiling with commiseration, Ace Fernandez made his next-to-last gesture in a misspent life. He reached for the pot.

As his eager hands shot out there was a sharp, tearing sound, and the white sleeve of the elder Fernandez ripped loudly, and there snugly against his arm was what is known in the parlance of those aware of such things as a sleeve holdout. In it were several cards, among them the missing nine, ten, and queen.

For one utterly appalling instant Ace Fernandez froze, with what sinking of the heart you can imagine. Then he made the second of his last two gestures. He reached for his gun.

It was, of course, the only thing left to do. Nobody from the Gulf to the Colorado would have denied it. Martin Jim, as we have said, wore a six-gun for use, and moreover he had rather strict notions about the etiquette of such matters as poker.

He looked, he saw, he reached. By the manner of presentation, it must not be inferred that these were separate actions. They were one.

His gun came level just as that of Señor Ace Fernandez cleared his holster, and Martin Jim fired twice right across the tabletop.

Lead, received in those proportions and with that emphasis and range is reliably reported to be indigestible.

The test of any theory is whether it works in practice, and science must record that theory as proved. They buried Señor Ace Fernandez with due ceremony, his full house pinned to his chest over the ugly blotch of blood, the torn sleeve and holdout still in evidence. If, in some distant age, his body is exhumed for scientific study, no poker player will look twice to ascertain the cause of death.

Now, as we have said, the Cactus Kid was giving no thought to the abrupt departure of Ace Fernandez, nor to the manner of his going. Nor did he think much about the fact that he might be considered a responsible party. The Kid was largely concerned with random thoughts anent the beauty and the grace of Bess O'Neal, the Irish and very pretty daughter of the ranching O'Neals, from beyond the Pecos.

It was the night of the big dance at Rock Creek

School, and Bess had looked with favor on his suggestion that he meet her at the dance and ride home with her. What plans were projected for the ride home have no part in this story. It is enough to say the Kid was enjoying the anticipation.

Twice, the Kid had agreed to meet Bess, and twice events had intervened. Once he had inadvertently interrupted a stage holdup and in the resulting exchange of comments had picked up a bullet in the thigh. Not a serious wound, but a painful one, so painful that he missed the dance and almost missed the funerals of the two departed stage robbers.

On the second occasion, someone had jestingly dared the Kid to rope a mountain lion. The Cactus Kid had never roped a lion and was scientifically interested in the possibilities. Also, he never refused a dare. He got a line on the cat, but the cat reversed himself in midair, hit the ground on its feet, and left the ground in that same breathtaking instant, taking a leap that put him right in the middle of the Kid's horse.

It is a scientifically accepted fact that two bodies cannot occupy the same place at the same time, and the resulting altercation, carried on while the frightened horse headed for the brush at a dead run, left the Kid a bedraggled winner.

His shirt was gone and he was smeared, head to foot with mingled lion and human blood. The Kid had handled the mountain lion with a razor-edged bowie knife, and regardless of their undoubted efficiency, they simply aren't neat.

Accordingly, Bess O'Neal, with Irish temper and considerable flashing of eyes and a couple of stamps of a dainty foot, had said he either must arrive on hand and in one piece or no more dates. Should he be in no condition to dance with her, he could go his way and she would go hers.

•   •   •

Hence, the Cactus Kid, wearing a black buckskin jacket heavily ornamented with silver, black-pearl inlaid gunbelt and holsters, black creased trousers, highly polished boots and a black, silver-ornamented sombrero, was bound for Rock Creek School.

His gelding, a beautiful piebald with a dark nose and one blue eye, stepped daintily along doing his best to live up to his resplendent master as well as to the magnificent saddle and bridle he wore.

These last had been created to order for Don Pedro Bedoya, of the Sonora Bedoyas, and stolen from him by one Sam Mawson, known to the trade as "One Gun" Mawson.

Mawson decided they would look best on the Kid's horse, and attempted to effect an exchange by trading a bullet in the head for the horse. He failed to make allowances for an Irishman's skull, and the bullet merely creased the Kid, who came to just as Mawson completed the job of exchanging saddles and was about to mount. The Cactus Kid spoke, Mawson wheeled and drew . . . One Gun was not enough.

The outlaw's taste, the Kid decided, was better than his judgment. He departed the scene astride a one-thousand-dollar saddle.

With Rock Creek School a bare six miles away where Bess O'Neal would be looking her most lovely, the Cactus Kid, a gorgeous picture of what every young cowhand would wear if he had money enough, rode along with a cheerful heart and his voice lifted in song.

"Lobo" Fernandez was big, rough, and ugly. He had loved his brother Ace—but then, Lobo never played poker with him. With Miguel, a younger brother, he waited beside the road. Someone had noticed and commented on that deft movement of the Kid's fingers that foretold the demise of Ace, and then, Lobo had never liked the Kid, anyway.

Out in the West, where men are men and guns are

understood, even the bravest of men stand quiet when an enemy has the drop. The Kid was a brave man, but Lobo and Miguel Fernandez, two men on opposite sides of the road, had the drop on him, and clearly the situation called for arbitration.

He reined in the piebald and for one heart-sinking, hopeless instant he realized this was the third and last chance given him by Bess O'Neal.

"Buenas noches, señores!" he said politely. "You go to the dance?"

"No!" Lobo was more emphatic than the occasion demanded. "We have wait for you. We have a leetle bet, Miguel and I, he bet the ants finish you before the buzzards. I say the buzzards weel do it first."

The Cactus Kid studied them warily. Neither gun wavered. If he moved he was going to take two big lead slugs through the brisket. "Let's forget it, shall we? The dance will be more fun. Besides, ants bother me."

There was no humor in the clan Fernandez. With hands bound behind him, and one Fernandez six feet on his left, another a dozen feet behind, the Cactus Kid rode away.

He knew what they planned, for the mention of ants was enough. It is a quaint old Yaqui custom to bind a victim to an anthill, and the Fernandez brothers had been suspected of just such action on at least two occasions. On one of these the Kid had helped to remove from the hill before the ants finished the body. It had been a thoroughly unpleasant and impressive sight.

The moon he had planned for Bess (by special arrangement) was undeniably gorgeous, the lonely ridges and stark boulders of the desert seemed a weird and fantastic landscape on some distant planet as the Cactus Kid rode down a dim trail guided by Lobo. Once, topping a rise, he glimpsed the distant lights of Rock Creek School, and even thought he heard strains of music.

The trail they followed dipped deep into the canyon of the Agua Prieta and skirted the dark waters of the

stream. The Cactus Kid knew then where they were taking him—to the old medicine camp of the Yaquis. With
the knowledge came an idea.

Suddenly Miguel sneezed, and when he did, his head
bobbed to the left.

"Ah!" the Kid said. "Bad luck! Very bad luck!"

"What?" Miguel turned his head to stare at him.

"To sneeze to the left—it's the worst kind of luck,"
the Kid said.

Neither Fernandez replied, yet he had a hunch the
comment on the old Yaqui superstition impressed them.
He knew it had been a belief of many of the southwestern
tribes that if the head bobbed left when one sneezed, it
spelled disaster. He had a hunch both men knew the old
belief.

"Tsk, tsk," he said softly.

Miguel shifted uncomfortably in the saddle. The high
black cliffs of the canyon loomed above them. Both men,
he knew, had been here before. Being part Yaqui, they
would be impressed with the evil spirits reported to
haunt the old medicine camp of the tribe.

He worked desperately with his cramped fingers, trying to get the rawhide thongs looser. A stone rattled
somewhere, and he jumped.

"What was that?" he said, in a startled voice.

Lobo Fernandez looked up, glared at him, then
glanced around uneasily. There was no moonlight here,
and nothing could be seen. The Kid's gun belt hung over
the pommel of Lobo's saddle, and with a free hand a lot
might be done.

"Wait!" he said suddenly, sharply.

The brothers reined in, and he could almost feel their
scowls. "Listen!" he said sharply. Their heads came up
with his word, and he had a hunch. When one listens for
something at night, there is invariably some sound, or
seeming sound.

Somewhere, rocks slid, and the canyon seemed to sigh. Lobo shifted uneasily in his saddle, and spoke rapidly to Miguel in Spanish, and Miguel grunted uneasily.

"Ah?" the Cactus Kid said. "You die soon."

"Huh?" Lobo turned on him.

"You die soon," the Kid repeated. "The Old Gods don't like you bringing me here. I'm no Yaqui. This here is a Yaqui place. A place of the spirits."

Lobo Fernandez ignored him, but Miguel seemed uneasy. He glanced at his brother as if to speak, then shrugged. The Kid worked at the rawhide thongs. His wrists were growing sweaty from the warmth and the constant straining. If he could get rid of them for a while, or if he had a little more time—

Then suddenly the trail widened and he was in the flat place beside the stream, the place where the Yaquis came, long ago. Once before, chasing wild horses, the Kid had been through here. There was an old altar, Aztec, some said, at the far end in a sort of cave formed by the overhang. The Mexican rider he had been with had been fearful of the place and wanted very much to leave.

"Maybe you die here," the Kid said. "My spirit say you'll die soon."

Lobo snarled at him, and then they halted. About here, the Kid recalled, there was a big anthill. They had certainly brought him to the right place, for no one would ever come by to release him. This was a place never visited by anyone. Probably only two or three white men had ever descended to this point, and yet it was no more than fifteen miles at most from Rock Creek School.

Lobo swung down, and then walked over to the Kid and, reaching up with one big hand, dragged him from the horse. The Kid shoved off hard and let go with all his hundred and forty pounds.

It was unexpected, and Lobo staggered and fell, cursing. Miguel sprang around the horse, and the Kid kicked out viciously with both feet and knocked the younger Fernandez rolling. But the Kid's success was short-lived.

Lobo sprang to his feet and kicked the Kid viciously in the ribs, and then they dragged him, cursing him all the while, to the anthill. He felt the swell of it under his back. Then, as they bound his feet and Miguel began to drive stakes in the ground, Lobo drew his knife and leaned over him. He made two quick gashes, neither of them deep, in either side of the Kid's neck.

Then he drew the sharp edge of the knife across the kid's stomach, making no effort to more than break the skin, and then on either of his ankles, after pulling off his boots. It was just something to draw enough blood to invite the ants. The rest they would accomplish in time, by themselves.

The two brothers drew off then, muttering between themselves. His talk of evil spirits had made them uneasy, he knew, and they kept casting glances toward the cave where the altar stood. Yet there seemed some other reason for their hesitation. They muttered among themselves, and then walked away, seeming to lose interest in him. Yet as they left he heard one word clearly above the others: *señorita.*

What señorita? He scowled, still struggling with the thongs that bound his ankles. They were growing slick from perspiration now, and perhaps some blood. The ants had not discovered him, and probably would not until morning brought them out.

He was lying across the anthill, lying on his side. Stakes driven into the ground on either side of his body, but some distance off, tied him in position so he could not roll away. The rawhide thongs binding him to the stakes were tight and strong. Other stakes had been driven into the ground above his head and below his feet. From the stake above his head a noose had been slipped under his jawbone and drawn tight, so his head was all but immovable. His ankles had been roped tight down to the stake below his feet.

It was with no happiness that the Cactus Kid contemplated his situation. Yet two factors aroused his curiosity; the señorita the brothers had talked about, and why they did not mount and leave the canyon.

Their work here had been done. Neither brother was immune from superstition, and in fact, both of them were ignorant men reared in all that strange tangle of fact and fancy that makes up Yaqui folklore. This place had a history, a weird history that extended back to some dim period long before the coming of the red man, back to those pre-Indian days when other peoples roamed this land.

Artifacts had been found in the caves, and back there where the idol was, there were stone remains of some kind of crude temple built under an overhanging shelf. A professor who explored the canyon had once told the Kid that the base of the supposedly Aztec god had provided a base for some other figure before it, that it was another type of stone, and one not found nearby.

Yet there was nothing in all this to help him. What he had hoped for, he did not know, but any uncertainty on their part could act favorably for him, so when the idea came to him, he had played on their superstition and the natural feeling all men have when in a strange, lonely place during the dark and silent hours. It had come to nothing. He was strapped to an anthill, and when the sun awakened them to full vigor and they began their work, they would find the blood, and then they would swarm over him by the thousands.

Doggedly, bitterly, almost without hope, he worked at the rawhide that bound his wrists. Fearful of what he might do if they had been freed even for a moment, the brothers Fernandez had left his hands tied when they threw him on the ground and staked him out. Yet despite the blood and perspiration on his chafed and painful wrists, the rawhide seemed loosened but little. Nevertheless, he continued to work, struggling against time and against pain.

Then suddenly, in a bitter and clarifying moment, he realized what they had meant when they spoke of a señorita. They had been talking about Bess.

The instant the idea came to him he knew he was right.

Not over a week ago when he rode up to her home and swung down from the saddle, she had told him about Lobo Fernandez and his brother, the smooth, polished one, the one called Juan. They had stopped her in front of the store and tried to talk. Juan had caught at her arm. She had twisted away, and then Ernie Cable had come out of the general store and wanted to know what was going on, and they had laughed and walked away. But she had noticed them watching the house.

They had been talking about Bess O'Neal. But *what*? What had they said?

Where were the other brothers? Where were Juan and Pedro?

The low murmur of voices came to him, and as he lay on the low mound of the anthill, he could see the glow of their cigarettes. They were sitting on the ground not far from the image, smoking. And waiting.

Using all his strength, he tugged at his bonds. They were solid, and they cut into his wrists like steel wire. He relaxed, panting. He could feel sweat running down his body under his shirt. This was going to be hell. Even if he got free, he still must get his hands on a gun, and even then, there would be four of them.

Four? There were only two, now. Yet once the idea had come to him, he couldn't get it out of his mind. Juan Fernandez was no fool. It was such a good chance, they could kill two birds with one stone. Juan wanted Bess O'Neal. If the Cactus Kid and Bess vanished at the same time, everyone would shrug and laugh. They would believe they had eloped. No one would even think to question the opinion. It was so natural a thing for them to do.

Revenge for their brother's death, and the girl. They

could take her to Sonora or back in the hills, and nobody would even think to look.

Then he heard the sound of horses on trail. He tried to lift his head to listen, but it was tied too tight. He lay there, hating himself and miserable, listening to the horses. Desperately, his mind fought for a way out, an escape. Again he strained his muscles against the binding rawhide. He forced his wrists with all his might, but although he strained until his hands dug into the sand under him, he could do nothing, he found them tight as ever. The sweat and blood made his wrists slippery so they would turn, ever so little, under the rawhide, but that was all.

His fingers were touching something, something cool and flat. For an instant, listening again to the approaching horses, that something made no impression, it refused to identify itself. Then on a sudden it hit him, and his fingers felt desperately.

A small, flat surface, light in weight, triangular—an arrowhead!

There were many of them here, he knew. All over this ancient medicine ground of the Yaqui Indians, delicately shaped from flint.

He gripped it in his fingers and tried to reach it up to the rawhide that bound his wrists.

They had crossed his wrists, then bound them tightly, and had taken several turns of the rawhide around his forearms, binding them tightly together, but by twisting his fingers he could bring the rawhide thong and the edge of the flint arrowhead together. Straining in every muscle, he commenced to saw at the thong.

The horses were still coming. In the echoing stillness of the canyon, he knew he would hear them for a good half hour before they arrived. The steep path was narrow, and they must come slowly.

Minutes passed. The cutting pain in his wrists was a gnawing agony now, and the salt of perspiration had mingled with it to add to his discomfort. Yet he struggled on. It was desperately hard to get the edge of the flint against the rawhide now, but he could still manage it, and a little pressure.

A voice called out, then another. The horses came into the basin, and he heard a question in Spanish, then a laughing response. Then a light was struck, and a fire blazed up. In the glow of the fire applied to sticks gathered earlier, he could see the four brothers, and Bess O'Neal.

She was standing with her back to him, her wrists tied, and Juan gripped her arm. Lobo stared at her greedily, and then Juan asked a question. Leading the girl, they turned toward the anthill and the Cactus Kid.

Bess cried out when she saw him. *"You!* When they told me you were here, I thought they lied. They said you were hurt—that you— Then when I was outside talking to them, I suddenly realized something was wrong, but when I tried to leave and go back inside to get someone else, they grabbed me, tied me, and brought me to this place."

"Keep your nerve, honey," the Cactus Kid said grimly. "This isn't over!"

Juan laughed and, leaning down, struck him across the mouth. "Pig!" he snarled. "I should kill you now. I should cut you to little pieces, only the ants will do it better. And if you die, you would not hear what happens to the señorita. It is better you hear!"

He straightened up, and they trooped back to the fire. The frightened, despairing look in the girl's eyes gave him added incentive. He scraped and scratched at the rawhide, staring hard toward the fire.

The brothers were in no hurry. They had the girl. They had him. He was helpless, and no one suspected them. Moreover, they were in a place where no one came. They could afford to take their time.

Suddenly he braced himself again and strained his muscles. He felt a sudden weakness in his bonds, and then his straining fingers found a loose end. He had cut through the rawhide!

Working with his swollen, clumsy fingers, he got the loose end looser, then managed to shake some of the other loops from his wrists. In a matter of minutes, his hands were free. He lay still then, panting and getting his wind, then he lifted his hands to the halter on his head and neck. A few minutes' work and that was freed, then the thongs that bound his wrists and ankles.

He was outside the glow of the fire, which was at least a hundred yards away. He chafed his swollen wrists and rubbed his hands together. Then he got several pieces of rawhide and stuck them into his pockets. One piece, about eighteen inches long, he kept.

The Cactus Kid got slowly to his feet, stretching himself, trying to get life into his muscles. In the vast, empty stillness of the black canyon the tiny fire glowed, and flamed red, and above it the soft voices, muted by distance and the enormity of the space around them, sounded almost like whispers.

Tiptoeing to the edge of the stream, he felt for the rock he wanted, two inches long and evenly balanced in weight. Taking the eighteen-inch rawhide, he knotted one end of it securely about the stone. Then he tried it in his hand.

Fading back into the shadows then, his boots still lying where Lobo had dropped them when they were jerked from his feet, the Kid melted into the almost solid blackness and began to cross the space between himself and the fire.

He didn't like killing, and he didn't like what he was going to have to do, yet he was not the one to underrate the fighting ability of the brothers Fernandez. They were cruel, vindictive men, lawless and given to murder. He knew what they would do to the girl, he knew the horror in which she would live for a few days or a few weeks, then murder. They dared not leave her alive, possibly to get back to Aragon.

To think that only a few miles away now, the dance was in progress! Only a few miles away old Buck Sorenson was calling dances and his sons were sawing their fiddles. There was help there, but it was too far. What was to be done, he must do himself.

Miguel knelt above the fire. He was cooking. Juan sat near the girl, and kept a hand on her. From time to time he made remarks to her in his sneering, irritating voice. Lobo sat across the fire, his eyes never leaving the girl's slim body or her face.

In the darkness, the Cactus Kid watched. His guns were there, he could see them lying on a blanket. They were too far away. There was no chance to get them.

He waited. It was a deadly, trying waiting. Minutes seemed like hours. Then Miguel straightened. "Pedro!" he snapped impatiently.

The Fernandez who dozed on the sand looked up.

"Get me some water from the spring, you lazy one!"

Pedro started to complain, then Juan looked up.

"Get it!" he snapped.

Grudgingly, Pedro picked up a canteen and started off into the darkness. The Cactus Kid came to his feet, moving like a ghost in his socked feet, moving after Pedro.

He waited, while the hulking Mexican held the canteen in the spring to fill it, and then as he straightened, the Kid moved in behind him, holding a loop of the rawhide in his left hand and gripping the stone in his fingers.

He threw the stone suddenly, and its weight swung the rawhide around the Mexican's neck. He had swung the stone from the right and with a quick, backhanded motion, and as it came around Pedro's neck the Kid caught it with his right. Then he jerked hard with both hands, cutting off the startled yell that started to rise in the man's throat, and gripping the rawhide hard, the Kid jerked his knee up into the small of Pedro's back and turned his knuckles hard against the back of Pedro's neck.

It was sudden, adroit, complete. For an instant the Kid held the man, then lowered him to the ground. Perhaps he was dead. Perhaps—there was no question now. Withdrawing the thong, the Kid searched him in vain for a gun, then slid away into darkness, and once more got close to the camp. He sighed regretfully. Pedro had been unarmed.

"Where is that fool, Pedro?" Miguel demanded impatiently. Then he yelled, *"Pedro!* Where are you?"

There was no answer.

The echo of Miguel's voice died, and for a minute the three brothers stared at each other. Lobo got to his feet, staring into the darkness. There was no sound out there but the falling water in the spring, and the rustle from the stream.

Lobo Fernandez shifted uneasily, staring around into the darkness. "I'll go see where is he," he said, finally.

Lying close, the Kid waited. What he wanted was a chance at those guns. Once the guns were in his hands, all would be well. Was he the Cactus Kid for nothing?

Lobo walked off into the darkness. Suddenly there was a startled yell from him.

"Juan!" Lobo screamed. "Come quickly! *Pedro is dead!"*

Juan Fernandez sprang to his feet and lunged toward Lobo's shouting voice. Miguel started up, his face ashen, and the Kid sprang, quickly, silently. Again the rawhide thong swung out, and again a man was jerked from his feet, but this time the Kid had no desire to kill.

"It is the spirits!" Lobo shouted. "The gringo told me they would be angry!"

Juan's shout broke in. "The Keed? He has done this! He has gotten away!"

The Cactus Kid heard them rushing toward the ant-hill where he had been tied, but he dropped the unconscious Miguel and sprang for the guns. He came up with the gun belt swinging in his hands and, with a quick movement, caught it and buckled the guns on. Then he sprang across the fire to the girl and dragged her into the darkness.

While she sobbed with relief he tore at the knots with frenzied, eager fingers.

"Where are the horses?" he said. "Get to them quickly! Get two and turn the others free. Then wait for me where the trail begins."

The girl asked no more questions, but slipped off into the darkness.

There was not a sound from the brothers. Miguel, his face blue, lay on the ground near the fire. He was not dead.

The Kid glided from behind the fire and, staring into the darkness, began to probe for the brothers Fernandez. Both were armed, as Pedro had not been. Both men were deadly with six-guns, and in any kind of a shoot-out they would be hard men to handle. Keeping his eyes away from the fire, he moved into the shadows, hoping to get near the horses, but out of line with the girl.

There was no sign from her. Then he heard a horse stamp and blow. He waited. Then he heard a footfall, so soft he scarce could hear. He whirled, gun in hand, and in the darkness he saw the looming figure of Lobo, just the faint outline of his figure in the light from the fire.

Their guns came up at the same instant, and both blasted fire. The Kid felt a quick stab at his side, not of pain, but rather a jolt as though someone had jerked him violently. Then he fired again, and saw the big figure of Lobo wilting, saw the gun dribble from his fingers, and at the same instant there was a scream from near the horses.

Turning in his tracks, he charged toward the scream and came up running. There was a wild scuffling in the dark, then a muttered curse and the sound of a blow. He saw them, and holstering his gun, the Kid lunged close and caught Juan with one hand at his shirt collar and one at his belt.

With a tremendous jerk, he ripped the Mexican free and shoved him violently away. With a cry, Juan turned like a cat in midair and hit the ground in a sitting position. He must have drawn as he fell, for suddenly his gun belched fire and then the Kid fired.

Juan Fernandez rolled over and the Kid dropped to the ground. They lay there, only a few feet apart, each waiting for a move from the other. Somewhere off to the right the girl was also lying still. Back at the fire Miguel might be coming to. What was to be done must be done now.

He could hear the horses moving, so evidently Bess had reached them safely again after he had pulled Juan away from her. All was quiet, and then he thought he detected a movement off to the right.

Picking up a small pebble, he tossed it into the water. It drew no fire, no reaction. Getting carefully to his feet, he tried to penetrate the darkness ahead of him. Circling, he headed toward where he believed Juan to be. Yet when he reached the spot, the outlaw was no longer there!

Glancing back toward the fire, he saw that Miguel, too, was gone.

Gun in hand, he started working toward the entrance to the trail where he had warned Bess to meet him.

The whereabouts of the brothers disturbed him. Their hatred over his responsibility, small as it had been, in the death of Ace, would be nothing at all now that he had escaped them, killed Pedro, and taken Bess O'Neal from them. Above all, once the two left this valley, the brothers Fernandez would know only too well their day around Aragon was over.

A movement near him, and he froze into a crouch, his gun lifted. Then he saw a dark shadow, and just as he lifted the gun and turned it toward the figure there came to his nostrils a faint, scarcely tangible breath of perfume!

A moment only he waited, then he took a chance. "Bess!" he hissed.

In a moment she was beside him. Her lips against his ear, she breathed softly. "Miguel is at the trail entrance! We cannot get away!"

"The horses?"

"I've yours and mine in the cutback under the shelf. Near that image!"

Taking her hand, he began to move on careful feet toward the place she mentioned. It was dark there, in the overhang of the cliff. He drew her to him and slipped his left arm around her waist. Freed from his bonds, with Bess O'Neal beside him, and his guns on his slim hips, the Cactus Kid was once more himself. Grimly, he waited.

Morning would come, and with it—well, the brothers Fernandez could run, or they could die, as they wished.

Dawn came, as dawns will, slipping in a gray mystery of beginning light along the far wall of the narrow canyon, then growing into light. The gray turned softer and lay down along the gravel bench. The ants, unaware of what they had missed, began to bestir themselves, and the Kid, seated against the wall with the head of Bess O'Neal on his shoulder, watched the light and was thankful.

No living thing beyond the ants appeared on the bench. He arose, and awakening the girl, they swung into the saddle and, walking their horses, started cautiously for the trail. When they rounded the cluster of boulders that concealed it from them, there was no one in sight. "Looks like they've gone!" he said.

"Not yet."

Juan Fernandez, sided by the younger Miguel,

stepped from the boulders at their side. Juan's eyes were hot with hatred, and the gun in his hand spoke clearly of what was to come.

"We are going to kill you, señor."

"Looks like it," the Kid said calmly. "Can I smoke first?"

Juan shrugged. "Why not? If your tobacco and papers are in your breast pocket?"

Very carefully, the Cactus Kid reached for them and built a cigarette.

"Too bad," he said, "a few more minutes and we'd have been in the clear." He put the cigarette in his mouth, then struck the match on the saddle. Holding it in his fingers, he grinned at Juan. "No offense," he said, "but I should have killed you last night. Still, they'll get you, the bunch at Aragon. They'll figure this out." The match was burning slowly. Too slowly. "Somebody must have seen you kidnap Bess."

"Nobody saw us," Juan said, with satisfaction. "If you are going to smoke, you better light that cigarette."

"Nevertheless," the Kid protested, "I think—" Then the flame of the match burned down to his fingers, and at the twinge of pain, he yelled "Ouch," and jerked back his hand, dropping the match.

Only his hand never stopped moving. He palmed his gun, and his gun bellowed with that of Juan Fernandez. The bullet of Juan cut a furrow across the saddle fork in front of him, but his own bullet slammed Juan in the chest and he staggered and fell to the sand even as the Cactus Kid's gun spoke another time.

Miguel let go his gun and grabbed at his side with an expression of shocked surprise in his eyes. He fell from the saddle and sprawled on his face in the sun. Juan tried to rise, then fell back.

Two hours and some twelve miles farther away toward the ranch where Bess lived with her uncle, the Cactus Kid tilted his sombrero back on his head and looked at Bess. Her eyes were bright and shining with promises. "You were very brave!" she said.

The Kid lifted a deprecating shoulder. "Not very," he said. "It wasn't that, but luck." Then, recalling in the flush of his success the ancient arrowhead, he added, "It was luck, and the Yaqui gods. They were with me, with us."

"Give them all the credit you want!" she insisted. "I think you're wonderful!"

The Cactus Kid smiled benevolently and brushed his fingernails lightly against the front of his shirt, then glanced at them.

"Of course," he said, "you may be right. Who am I to argue with a lady?"

VALLEY OF THE SUN

Sprawled on his face beside the cholla, the man was not dead. The gun that lay near his hand had not been fired. He lay now as he had fallen six hours earlier when the two bullets struck him. But the dark stain on the back of his sun-faded shirt was from blood that had caked hard, dried in the blasting sun.

Above him, like the tower of a feudal castle, was the soaring height of Rattlesnake Butte. It loomed like a sentinel above the sun-tortured waste of the valley.

Near the wounded man's hand a tiny lizard stopped. Its heart throbbed noticeably through the skin as it stared in mingled amazement and alarm at the sprawled figure of the man. It sensed the warning of danger in the stale smell of sweat and blood.

Under the baking heat of the sun, the man's back muscles stirred. The lizard darted away, losing itself in a tiny maze of rocks and ruined mesquite. But the muscles of the wounded man, having stirred themselves, relaxed once more and he lay still. Yet the tiny movement, slight as it had been, seemed to start the life processes functioning again. Little by little, as water finds its way through rocks, consciousness began to trickle back into his brain.

His eyes were open a long time before he became aware of his position. At first, he merely lay there, his mind a complete blank, until finally the incongruity of his stillness filtered into his mind and stirred him to wonder as to the cause.

Then memory broke the dam caused by bullet shock and flooded him suddenly.

He knew then that he had been shot. Understanding the manner of men who fired upon him, he knew also that they had left him for dead. He was immediately aware of the advantage this gave him.

Mentally, he explored his body. He was wounded, but where and how he did not know. From the dull throb in his skull he suspected at least one bullet must have hit him in the head. There was, he discovered, a stiffness low down on his left side.

He could remain here no longer. He must first get out of the sun. Then he must take stock of his position and decide what was to be done. Being a desert man, he was acutely aware of the danger of lying in the sun and having all the water drawn from his body. There was a greater danger from heat and thirst than from men determined to kill him.

Brett Larane got his hands under him and very carefully pushed himself up. He flexed his knees with great caution. His arms and legs functioned normally, which was a good sign. To be helpless now would mean sure death.

When he was on his knees he lifted a hand to the scalp wound in his head. It was just that, no more nor less. No doubt there had been a mild concussion also. The wound in his lower left side was worse, and from the caked condition of his shirt and pants, he knew he must have lost a great deal of blood.

Bleeding, he knew, would make a man thirsty, and this was an added danger.

He retrieved his gun and returned it to his holster. The shot that struck him down had come utterly without warning. The drawing of the gun had been one of those purely instinctive actions, natural to a man who is much dependent upon a weapon. It had been due to conditioning rather than intelligence.

Shakily, he got to his feet and glanced around for his horse, but it was nowhere in sight.

They had taken his outfit, then. He was a man afoot in the desert, miles from possible aid, a man who had lost his saddle. In this country, that alone was tantamount to a death sentence.

There was shade under the overhang of the butte and he moved toward it, walking carefully. Once there, he lowered himself gingerly to a sitting position. He was afraid of opening the wound and starting the bleeding again. Weakness flooded him, and he sat there, gasping and half-sick with fear. Nausea swept over him and came up in his throat.

He wanted to live, he wanted desperately to live.

He wanted to see Marta once more, to finish the job he had begun for her. He wanted to repay those who had shot him down from ambush. He wanted all these things, and not to die here alone in the shadow of a lost butte on a sun-parched desert.

Realist that he was, he knew his chances of survival were slight. On this desert without a horse, a strong man might figure the odds as at least fifty to one against him. For a wounded man, the odds went to such figures that they were beyond the grasp of any run-of-the-herd cowhand.

Horse Springs, the last settlement, lay sixty miles behind him. And in this heat and without water, that distance made the town as remote as a distant planet. Willow Valley lay some forty or fifty miles ahead, somewhere over yonder in the blue haze that shrouded the mountains along the horizon.

No doubt there was water not too far distant, but in what direction and how far?

There are few stretches of desert without some sort of spring or water hole. But unless one knew their location they were of no use, for no man could wander about at random hoping to find one. One might be within a dozen yards of one and never know it.

All the while he thought of this he knew he dared not look. He would have no direction, no indication, and in his condition there was but one thing, to head for Willow Valley and hope someone found him before he died.

Nor was the trail one often traveled. Outlaws like those who shot him infested this country. Few people wanted to go to Horse Springs, so the desert was avoided. He had taken this road for that purpose, never dreaming that Joe Creet would guess the route he had chosen.

It had been Creet, of course, who shot him. Larane had heard his jeering voice in the momentary space that separated the shots.

He had seen the three riders from the Saxon Hills in one fleeting glimpse as he tumbled from the saddle, and he would not soon forget their faces. Joe Creet, Indian Frank, and Gay Tomason.

Trouble had been building for some time between Creet and himself, but it was Tomason's presence there that surprised him. An expression of cold triumph was on the man's face as he lifted his gun.

Joe Creet's motive was obvious enough. The outlaw had always hated him. Only six weeks ago he had given Creet a beating that left marks still visible on the man's face. Moreover, Creet must have learned about Marta Malone's money, which he had been carrying.

But Tomason?

Gay had been his friend, they had ridden together, worked together, come west together.

The answer to that was Marta. With him out of the running, Gay would have the inside track with her. With no other eligible men around, Gay would probably win her. For a long time Brett Larane had been aware of Gay's interest in the girl, but he had never believed it would go this far.

•　　•　　•

Larane was a quiet man, tall and strong, and given to deep, abiding loyalties and lasting friendships.

It would have been Gay who told Creet what trail he was to take. Creet could have trailed him, but could not have been lying in wait for him as he had been, so Tomason must have told Creet or even led him to the spot. Yet with both men, and with Indian Frank, who followed wherever Creet led, the motive lay deeper than these more obvious things.

No one needed to tell Brett Larane of the seriousness of his position. In this heat a man without water, by resting in the shade at all times, might live from two to five days. Traveling by night and resting in the shade by day, he might live from one to three days, and might make twenty miles. And twenty miles would leave him exactly nowhere.

Yet if he was to survive, he must make an effort. Here in the shade of Rattlesnake Butte he could not afford to wait. Time was precious, and he must move on. And well he knew that all of those calculations on time and distance concerned a man in the full flower of health, and he was wounded and weak.

For the time at least, he must wait. To start in the sun would finish him within a few miles at most.

Sweat trickled down his face, and he fanned himself weakly with his hat. He felt faint and sick now, all his rugged strength seeming to drain away. He tried not to think of the thirst that was already drying his throat and cracking his parched lips. He thought of Marta Malone, and the Hidden Valley Ranch.

It was a small ranch, lonely and yet beautiful, nestling in the shoulder of the mountains that somebody had named Hidden Valley. A pleasant place, a place where he had thought to live out his life with Marta.

That had been his one thought, ever since he drifted into the Valley of the Sun and went to work for her, first as a puncher, and then when they all quit, as foreman of a ranch without hands. But he had worked on. He had dammed the spring and formed a pool, he had repaired the house and built an adobe barn. He had broken fifteen wild horses, branded cattle, and kept at it, doing everything possible without thought of reward.

Hiring some drifting cowhands, he had taken her herd to the stock pens at Horse Springs and sold them to a stock buyer for a good price, the first returns that Marta had won from the ranch since her father died. And then he had been robbed.

The worst of it was, they would probably tell her he had run off with her money, and she would have little choice but to believe them.

His head throbbed with dull pain, and the angry teeth of a more raw and bitter pain gnawed at his wounded side. He knew that his wounds should be washed and cleansed, but he had no water, and there was nothing he could do.

The day drew on and the band of shadow in which he sat narrowed. The stifling heat danced upon the far length of the desert. Dust devils moved in a queer rigadoon across the levels. Heat beat down upon him, but at last his eyes closed and he slept. His face greasy with sweat, his body stiff with the torture from his wounds.

A buzzard circled in the sky, and then another came near, and a long time later Brett opened his eyes. Weakly, he pushed himself erect, staring with dazed eyes over the gathering of shadows around him, and the red-and-gold-tipped peaks of the far-off mountains. It would soon be time to move.

Automatically, he felt for his gun. One shot, and then he would need to worry no more. Just one, and then no more pain, no more trouble. Yet even as he thought of it he remembered the beauty of Marta, awaiting him in the doorway at Hidden Valley, her hand shading her eyes, then a smile, and she would come running down the steps. In these past months they had drawn very close to one another.

He looked down at the gun. They had left him that,

never guessing he would have the chance to use it again, and he might not.

Marta needed that money. Her whole existence at Hidden Valley depended on it. Only his efforts had enabled her to gather the cattle and get them on the road to market. Without him and the money she could do nothing. And because he had trusted Gay, she would trust him.

Brett Larane felt with a thick and fumbling tongue for the parched and cracked lips. Then he got a finger hold in a crevice of the rock and looked out at the desert. The sun was gone now, and a vague coolness seemed to drift over the desert. He turned and braced himself, gathering his strength. Then he pushed away from the cliff and began to walk.

He was weak, but he kept his eyes on the mountains and moved along steadily. When he had walked a half mile he paused and seated himself carefully on a rock, resting. Nearby there was a mesquite root that would do for a cane. After ten minutes he got up and started on.

Darkness closed around him and he kept moving. Once, far off over the desert, he heard a coyote howl, and once a rabbit scurried by him, dodging away through the rocks and cholla.

He walked on and on, resting at intervals, but continuing to push on. Once, he stumbled and was too weak to rise for a long time. So he lay sprawled out on the desert, his body deliciously cool and relaxed even while his throat burned with thirst.

When he opened his eyes the sky was faintly gray in the east. He struggled to his feet and started on.

Now he must find shelter from the sun. He must find something, somehow, nearby. He would make no more than a couple of miles at his present pace before the sun was up. Yet there was nothing in sight and he pushed on. Suddenly the face of the desert was broken by the sandy scar of a wash. It came down from low hills, and he followed along the lip, walking away from his trail, for often along a wash one might find water.

The sun was looking over the horizon when he glimpsed the green of a cottonwood. His tongue was swollen, but felt thick and dry. He pushed on, then hearing a noise in the brush close to the base of the slim young cottonwood, he halted and, creeping closer, peered through.

Two porcupines were digging industriously into the sand, and he waited for a minute, watching, and then seeing damp sand being scraped from the hole they were digging, he moved up and drove them away.

Water!

He fell on his knees and dug eagerly into the damp sand at the bottom of the hole, and soon it grew sloppy and muddy, and then he sat back, letting the water seep through into the hole. It was still muddy when he cupped his hand into it and lifted it to his lips. He managed to get a swallow, then moistened his lips and tongue with his damp hand.

All day he waited beside the hole, drinking from time to time, and resting in the flimsy shade of the cottonwood. Toward dusk he bathed his head and face. Then he bathed the raw wound in his side. Having nothing with which to bandage it, he took some green leaves, dipped them in water, and bound them on, using his handkerchief for a compress and a pigging string from his hip pocket to secure the makeshift dressing.

He was picking up his cane to go when he heard a movement in the brush. He froze, and his gun slid into his hand. There was the sound of a horse's hoof striking stone, and then the brush was thrust apart and a horse walked through, a horse with an empty saddle!

His heart gave a leap. "Buck!" he gasped joyfully. "Well, I'll be darned!"

The horse jerked his head up and stopped. He spoke again, and the animal thrust a wary nose out toward him, sniffing curiously of his hand, but not liking the smell of blood that lingered in the air. Brett got his hand on the bridle and led the horse to the small spring, scarcely more than a bucket of water in sight.

Obviously, the horse had escaped, running away when Brett was fired upon, and then the animal, probably headed toward home and browsing along the way, had smelled water. When the horse had drunk, Brett Larane pulled himself into the saddle and started for the trail.

As he rode he studied his situation. He was very weak, and the distance he had to go was great. Yet by resting from time to time he believed he could make it if the wound in his side did not again begin to bleed.

It was not only essential that he arrive at the ranch but that he reach it in condition to act. He had no doubt that if Gay Tomason and Creet were not already there, they soon would be. There was no aid anywhere near for Marta, even if she wished to protest whatever steps they might take. But the chances were that Tomason would go to her as a friend. And even if she knew much of what Joe Creet and Indian Frank were, she had believed that Tomason was a friend.

Darkness was falling when Brett rode the buckskin off the trail into the piñons along the mountainside. Buck pulled against his guiding hand, wanting the home corral and the feed that awaited him there. But Brett rode him up through the trees, skirting along a dim cattle trail until he could come down upon the Hidden Valley Ranch from behind, riding down through the aspens.

A light shone from the window of the small ranch house, and his eyes narrowed with thought as he saw another light come on in his own cabin, which had formerly served as the bunkhouse. They were there, then. Tomason was there, and probably Creet.

They had Marta's money, and now they wanted her ranch, and probably her.

He wondered if Tomason had thought of Creet and the girl. With his shrewd eyes, Brett had long been aware of Creet's desire for the girl, and he had watched the man speculatively appraising Marta on more than one occasion. Tomason, for all his gun skill, was no match for Creet.

The outlaw was a cold-blooded killer, and he was a deadly hand with a six-gun. Only Brett Larane might match him in gunplay, and of that fact only two men were aware—Larane himself, and Joe Creet.

Creet knew that Larane had a reputation in Hays and Tascosa, a fact unknown to Tomason or to any of the others in the Valley of the Sun country or the Saxon Hills. Larane had backed down the Catfish Kid on two occasions, and Jesse Evans, Billy the Kid's former pal and later enemy, had backed down for him. In that tough and hard-bitten crowd that included Hendry Brown, Frank Valley, and Dave Rudabaugh, Brett Larane had been left strictly alone.

Two things he must do now. He must at all costs recover the money for Marta, and he must kill Joe Creet and Gay Tomason.

Had he been a well man, he might have handled the situation without gunfire. But in his present shape, with no knowledge of how long he would be around, he dared take no chances. If he did not live, he must be sure that the others died. And he must be sure that if he was to be sick or crippled, none of the three were around to take advantage of his and the girl's helplessness.

He knew the risk he was taking, but at all costs he had to have water. He had ridden for hours now without a drink, and the water earlier had scarcely been sufficient to refresh him after his long thirst. Moreover, he must know who was at the ranch, and what was happening there.

Leaving the buckskin tethered in the aspens, he moved carefully toward the ranch house.

At the spring he lowered himself to the ground and drank long and deeply. Lifting his head, he studied the situation with care, then turned toward the bunkhouse. He must first know who was on the grounds. At a window, flattened against the side of the building, he glanced within.

Joe Creet was hunched over the table, and Indian Frank sat on the edge of a bunk. Gay Tomason was tipped back against the wall in a chair. "What I say"—Tomason was speaking—"is we split the money now. Then you hombres take a good-sized herd and leave me here. That's fair enough."

Creet's dry chuckle was a warning to Brett Larane, who knew his man, but Gay saw nothing in it. "Sure, that's fair enough," Joe agreed, "in fact, that's more than fair. But who wants to be fair?"

Tomason's smile faded. "Well, let's have your idea, then!" he demanded sharply. "I've stated my case."

"My idea?" Creet chuckled again, and his small black eyes were pinned on Tomason with contempt. "I want the money, and the girl."

Tomason's chair legs hit the floor, his face was dark with angry blood. "She's mine!" he said furiously. "She's in love with me, and she wants me! She doesn't enter into this!"

"Doesn't she?" Creet sneered. "I say she does. I'd kill"—he stared at Tomason—"for a woman like that as quick as for money. I'd even kill you, Gay."

Their eyes held, and Brett watched, fascinated. He saw what was in Creet's mind, and he could sense the evil triumph within the man at this moment. Joe Creet liked nothing and hated everything. He was a man eaten by a cancer of jealousy and hatred, and now he was savoring his triumph over the handsome Gay Tomason.

"So? That's the way it is?" Larane knew what Tomason was going to do. The man did have courage, of a kind, and now he laughed suddenly. "Why, I might have guessed you'd never play fair with any man, Joe! I might have known that as soon as I helped you put Brett out of the way, I would come next.

"I see things different, myself. I wouldn't kill for any woman. You can have her. Now, if you like."

Tomason chuckled as he finished speaking, and leaned his elbows on his knees. "Let's forget her and split the money. If you insist on Marta, there's no reason for me staying around."

"Sure." Joe Creet got up slowly, smiling with hard eyes. "I think that's just what I'll do. Go up an' see her now." He turned on his heel with a last sneering glance at Gay, and stepped toward the door.

It was a trap, but Tomason was too intent on his own subterfuge, for as Creet's back turned to him Gay Tomason went for his gun and started to his feet in the same moment. And then Indian Frank buried his knife to the haft in the back of Tomason's neck!

The big cowhand gasped, his mouth opening and closing. He tried to lift his gun. But at the grunt of Indian Frank as he drove home the knife, Creet wheeled like a cat and shattered Gay's wrist with a sweeping blow of his gun barrel. Tomason's gun crashed to the floor, and the cowhand stood swaying, then his knees buckled under him, and he went down. Deliberately, Creet kicked him in the stomach, then the face.

"Good job," Creet said, grinning at his crony. "Now we'll have the money, and the girl." He looked up at the Indian. "And I mean both of us. Let's eat, and then we'll go up."

Carefully, Brett Larane eased away from the cabin wall. On cat feet he started for the house, and when he got to the door, he tried the knob. It was not locked. Opening it, he stepped in.

Marta heard the creak of the door and looked up. Her

eyes went wide in startled horror. He lifted his finger to his lips. Then he got to the table and dropped into a chair. In gasping words, he told her of the shooting on the trail, of his own wounds, and of the murder of Gay Tomason.

His face was deathly pale, and he felt sick and empty. He tried holding his hands steady, and his lips stiffened as he felt them tremble. He could never hope to shoot accurately enough to kill both men before they got him. He needed time—time. And there was no time. They were coming now, in just a few minutes.

Yet there was a chance. If he could keep them in the cabin, prevent them from getting out . . . He looked up. "Where's my rifle?" he asked hoarsely. With the rifle he could pin them down, hold them back, possibly kill them at a distance. Away from Marta.

"They took it, Brett. Creet came in with Gay, said there was a coyote he wanted to kill. There isn't a gun in the house except the one you're wearing."

For money and a girl . . . they believed they had killed him, they knew they had killed Gay. They would stop at nothing, and they had been sure Marta had no weapons. The minutes fled, and he stared wildly from the girl to the window, trying desperately to think. Some way to stop them! There had to be a way! There just had to be!

His dwindling strength had mostly been dissipated on the long ride home. He knew, with an awful fear for Marta, that he could never get to the bunkhouse again. He doubted if he could cross the room. The sweat stood out on his face, and in the pale light he looked ghastly.

Slumped in the chair, his breath came in long gasps. His head throbbed, and the rat's teeth of agony bit into his side. He tried to force his fevered mind to function, to wrest from it one idea, anything, that might help.

When Creet saw him there, he was going to shoot. The outlaw would give him no chance to plan, to think. Nor would he hesitate. Creet knew him too well. He would, at first glimpse, realize Brett Larane's tragic weakness. There would be no second chance. Joe Creet must die before he cleared the doorstep, while he was stepping across it. Brett frowned against the pain, and his thoughts struggled with the problem.

He had no strength to lift a gun, no strength to hold a gun even, nor did he dare risk Marta's life by allowing her to use his gun. There was in his mind no thought of fair play, for there was nothing fair about any of this. It was murder, ugly and brutal, that they planned.

They had not thought of fair play when they ambushed him. Creet hadn't thought of fair play when he lured Gay Tomason into a chance at his back while Indian Frank sneaked up with his knife. If he was to save Marta and the ranch he had worked for, it must be now, and by any means.

Then he saw the box. It was a narrow wooden box, quite heavy, with rope handles. He had seen such boxes often used for carrying bar gold. The handles were inch-thick rope in this case, the ends run through holes and held on the inside by knots.

"Marta," he whispered hoarsely, "break the near end out of that box. Force the nails without noise, if you can."

He sat at the table and stared as she worked, and in a few minutes she had the end removed. "Now, from the other end," he whispered. "Cut the rope handle out and put the box on the table!"

Wondering, she did so, and looked at him curiously as he fumbled with the box to move it, the long way toward the door, the open end toward him. "Now," he said softly, "my gun."

Drawing it carefully from its worn holster, Marta placed it on the table beside him. Lifting the gun, he gripped the butt and pushed his arm and hand into the box, which was open on top. Marta, her eyes suddenly bright, caught his intention, and guided the muzzle of the barrel to one of the holes from which the rope had been taken. It was just large enough to take the muzzle of the six-gun.

"Now," he said, looking up at her, "throw a cloth over it, like it was food or something, covered on the table."

His hand gripping the butt on the gun, and the box covered by the cloth, Brett Larane sat facing the door, waiting. They would come, and they would come soon, and he had the gun fixed now, in position, pointed directly at the door. And he needed no strength to hold it ready for firing . . . but he had to get that first shot, while Joe Creet was in range, and he had to kill with that first shot. Afterward, Indian Frank might run off, or he might try to come through the door. If he came through the door, he, too, would die.

"Will you be all right, Brett?" Marta asked him gently.

He nodded, liking the feel of her hand on his shoulder. "Only, I hope they come . . . soon."

She left him to put coffee on the stove, and his eyes strayed toward the door, knowing as well as she, what little chance they had. He must make desperately sure of that first shot. Indian Frank was not dangerous without Creet, but the outlaw would be dangerous at any time.

She glanced from the window, but shook her head, and Brett sipped the coffee she offered him, a little at a time. His left hand trembled so, she had to hold the cup to his lips. He drank, then managed a few swallows of food.

They came silently and were scarcely heard. A quick grasp on his shoulder and Brett opened his eyes, aware for the first time that he had fallen asleep. His heart pounding, he gripped the gun butt and his finger slid through the trigger guard. And then the door opened.

It was Creet, but even as Brett Larane's finger tightened on the trigger, Joe turned sidewise and motioned to Indian Frank. "Come in!" he said, and then his head swung toward the room.

For the first time he saw the man sitting across the table beyond the coal-oil lamp. He jumped as if shot, and his hand swept down for his gun, but at that instant, Indian Frank stepped into the doorway. Brett squeezed the trigger, and the concealed gun bellowed loud in the silent room.

Frank, caught in midstep, stopped dead still, then sprawled facedown in the doorway, and Joe Creet leaped aside. Brett's second shot, booming hollowly, lost itself through the open door.

Creet, gun in hand, stared at him. "Well, I'm forever damned!" he said softly. "You're a hard one to kill, Larane! A hard one! I'd have sworn you were dead back there, with blood all over you! And now you've got Frank . . . well, that saves me the trouble. I never figured on him sharing the money. I had plans for him."

He looked at the table and the cloth-covered box. "Whatever you've got there, I don't know," he said, his eyes wary, "but you'd never be settin' that way, your hand covered an' all, if you could hold a gun. You'd never have missed the second shot you fired. Nor would you be settin' there now. You'd have turned that gun on me.

"No, I reckon you're not dead, but you're not quite alive, either. You're hurt bad."

The outlaw's face was saturnine, and his eyes were wicked with triumph. "Well, well! I'm glad to see you, Larane! Always did sort of spoil my fun, thinkin' you wouldn't be here to watch."

Brett's fingers tightened on the gun butt, trying to ease it out of the hole in the box, but it would not come loose, or his strength was too little to exert the necessary pull.

"Come over here!" Creet looked up at Marta. "Come over here and do what I tell you, or I'll drill him right through the head."

Marta Malone, transfixed with horror, stared from Creet's tense, evil features to the poised gun in his hand. Then, as if walking in her sleep, she started to move toward him.

Brett Larane stared at Creet, too weak to lift a hand, helpless to prevent the outlaw from doing as he wished.

Suddenly, something clicked in his brain. It was a wild, desperate, impossible chance—but there was no other choice.

"Marta—!" he said, speaking as loudly as he could. *"Think!"*

"Shut up!" Creet snarled at him. "Shut up or I'll brain you!"

"Think, Marta!" Brett begged. "Please think! Marta . . . !" His voice lifted as she drew near Creet. "Think—*the door!"*

As if he had spoken his thought, Marta understood, and with all her strength she hurled herself at the side of the gunman! Her weight hit him, and he staggered. His gun blasted a stab of flame, and a dish across the room crashed into bits as Joe Creet went staggering into the open doorway!

As he hit the doorpost with his shoulder he ripped his next shot out, and the lamp beside Brett shattered into bits, splashing him with oil, and then his own gun bellowed, and the dark figure in the doorway jerked spasmodically. Brett triggered the gun again, and the outlaw screamed . . . then broke his scream off in a choking, rattling sound, drowned by Brett Larane's last shot.

Joe Creet, hit three times, toppled forward and sprawled on his face outside the door. For a moment, in a deathly silence, they could hear the scratching of his fingers on the hard-packed earth beyond the step. Scratching, and then silence, a lonely shuddering silence in which Marta Malone clasped Brett Larane's head against her breast and sobbed brokenly in relief and shock.

There was sunlight in his face when he opened his eyes, sunlight, but he liked it, enjoyed it.

He looked around, remembering Marta's room, and seeing the sharp, bright, cleanliness of it, and the look of home about it.

The door opened as he lay there, enjoying the warmth and peace of it, and knowing it was early morning, and that he felt good.

The door opened, and Marta came in, her face bright when she saw he was awake. "Oh, Brett! You're up at last! I thought you would never awaken! How do you feel?" She put her hand on his face. He caught it and held it, looking up at her. "Like I never wanted to leave!" he said, smiling. "But what happened?"

"Nothing, until the next morning. Then a man came out from Willow Springs to get some money I owed him, and he buried the bodies and then he went in and sent the doctor out. I found the money they had stolen in Joe Creet's saddlebags in the bunkhouse."

"Better not think about it," he said quietly. "Tomorrow it will be an old story."

"Tomorrow, Brett? Why, it's already been more than two weeks! You've been awfully sick! Your side . . . the doctor said if it hadn't had care right away, you would have died!"

"Well, I didn't. Now we've got work to do. I'll have to find a crew, and—"

"We've got a bunch of boys, Brett. The doctor hired them for me, four of them, Texas men who were heading back after a cattle drive. You'll have a crew to boss when you can get around again!"

"And I suppose they are all flirting with you!" he said darkly. "I reckon it is time I got around!"

"No, they haven't flirted—much. The doctor told them we were going to be married."

"Oh, he did, did he? And what did you say?"

"Why, what could I say? He was such a nice man, and had been so helpful, I just couldn't have all those cowhands thinking he lied, could I?"

Brett Larane sank back against the pillow and grinned weakly. "You sure couldn't!" he said. "You sure couldn't!"

THAT SLASH SEVEN KID

J ohnny Lyle rode up to the bog camp at Seep Spring just before noon. Bert Ramsey, foreman of the Slash Seven outfit, glanced up and nodded briefly. Ramsey had troubles enough without having this brash youngster around.

"Say!" Johnny hooked a leg around the saddle horn. "Who's this Hook Lacey?"

Ramsey stopped walking. "Hook Lacey," he said, "is just about the toughest hombre around here, that's all. He's a rustler and a horse thief, and the fastest hand with a gun in this part of the country since Garrett shot Billy the Kid."

"Ride alone?"

"Naw. He's got him a gang nigh as mean as he is. Nobody wants any part of them."

"You mean you let 'em get away with rustling? We'd never cotton to that back on the Nueces."

Ramsey turned away irritably. "This ain't the Nueces. If you want to be useful why don't you go help Gar Mullins? The heel flies are driving cows into that quicksand faster'n he can drag 'em out."

"Sure." Johnny Lyle swung his leg back over the saddle. "Only I'd rather go after Lacey and his outfit."

"*What?*" Ramsey turned on him. "Are you crazy? Those hombres, any one of 'em, would eat three like you for breakfast! If that bunch tackles us, we'll fight, but we'll not go huntin' 'em!"

"You mean you don't want me to."

Ramsey was disgusted. What did this kid think he was doing, anyway? Like a fool kid, to make a big play in front of the hands, who were listening, to impress them how tough he was. Well, there was a way to stop *that!*

"Why, no," he said dryly. "If you want to go after those outlaws after you help Gar get the cattle out of the quicksand, go ahead."

Sundown was an hour past when Gar Mullins rode up to the corral at the Slash Seven. He stripped the saddle from his bronc, and after a quick splash and a wipe, he went in and dropped on a bench at the table. Old Tom West, the owner, looked up.

"Where's the kid?" he asked. "Where's my nephew? Didn't he come in?"

Gar was surprised. He glanced around the table.

"Shucks, ain't he here? He left me about three o'clock or so. Said Bert told him he could get Hook Lacey if he finished in time."

"*What!*" Tom West's voice was a bull bellow. His under jaw shot out. "Bert, did you tell him that?"

Ramsey's face grew red, then pale. "Now, look, boss," he protested, "I figured he was talking to hear hisself make a big noise. I told him when he helped Gar get all them cows out, he could go after Lacey. I never thought he'd be fool enough to do it."

"Aw!" Chuck Allen grinned. "He's probably just rode into town! Where would he look for that outfit? And how could he find 'em when we ain't been able to?"

"We ain't looked any too hard," Mullins said. "I know I ain't."

Tom West was silent. At last he spoke. "Nope, could never find 'em. But if anything happens to that boy, I'd never dare look my sister in the face again." He glared at Bert Ramsey. "If anything does happen to him you'd better be halfway to the border before I hear it."

Johnny Lyle was a cheerful, easygoing, free-talking youngster. He was pushing eighteen, almost a man by Western standards, and as old as Billy the Kid when Billy was leading one of the forces in the Lincoln County War.

But Johnny was more than a brash, devil-may-care youngster. He had been born and raised on the Nueces, and had cut his riding teeth in the black chaparral between the Nueces and the Rio Grande. When his father died he had been fourteen, and his mother had moved east. Johnny had continued to hunt and wander in the woods of the Virginia mountains, but he had gone to New York several times each month.

In New York he had spent a lot of time in shooting galleries. In the woods he had hunted, tracked, and enjoyed fistic battles with rugged mountaineers. He had practiced drawing in front of a mirror until he was greased lightning with a gun. The shooting galleries gave him the marksmanship, and in the woods he had learned to become even more of a tracker than he had learned to be in the brush country of his father, to which he returned for his summer vacations.

Moreover, he had been listening as well as talking. Since he had been here on the Slash Seven, Gar Mullins had several times mentioned the rough country of Tierra Blanca Canyon as a likely hangout for the rustlers. It was believed they disposed of many stolen cattle in the mining camps to the north, having a steady market for beef at Victorio and in the vicinity.

Tom West loved his sister and had a deep affection for his friendly, likable nephew, but Johnny was well aware that Tom also considered him a guest, and not a hand. Mullins could have told them the kid was both a roper and a rider, and had a lot of cow savvy, but Mullins rarely talked and never volunteered anything.

Johnny naturally liked to be accepted as an equal of the others, and it irritated him that his uncle treated him like a visiting tenderfoot. And because he was irked, Johnny decided to show them, once and for all.

Bert Ramsey's irritable toleration of him angered him.

Once he left Mullins, when the cattle were out of the quicksand, he headed across the country through Sibley Gap. He passed through the gap at sundown and made camp at a spring a few miles beyond. It could be no more than seven or eight miles farther to the canyon of which Mullins had talked, for he was already on the Tierra Blanca.

At daybreak he was riding. On a sudden inspiration, he swung north and cut over into the trail for Victorio.

The mining town had the reputation of being a rugged spot, and intended to keep it. The town was named after the Apache chieftain who had several times taken a bad whipping trying to capture the place. Several thousand miners, gamblers, gunmen, and outlaws made the place a good one to steer clear of. But Johnny Lyle had not forgotten the talk about Slash Seven beefs being sold there by rustlers.

Johnny swung down from his horse in front of the Gold Pan Restaurant and walked back to a corral where he saw several beef hides hanging. The brand was Seven Seventy-seven, but when he turned the hide over he could see it had been changed from a Slash Seven.

"Hey!" A bellow from the door brought his head up. "Git away from those hides!"

The man was big. He had shoulders like the top of an upright piano and a seamed and battered face.

Johnny walked to the next hide and the next while the man watched. Of the five fresh hides, three of them were Slash Sevens. He turned just in time to meet the rushing butcher.

Butch Jensen was big, but he was no mean rough-

and-tumble scrapper. This cowhand was going to learn a thing or two.

"I told you to get away!" he shouted angrily, and drew back his fist.

That was his first mistake, for Johnny had learned a little about fighting while in New York. One thing was to hit from where your fist was. Johnny's fist was rubbing his chin when Jensen drew his fist back, and Johnny punched straight and hard, stepping in with the left.

The punch was short, wicked, and explosive. Jensen's lips mashed under hard knuckles and his hands came up. As they lifted, Johnny turned on the ball of his left foot and the toe of his right, and whipped a wicked right uppercut into Jensen's huge stomach.

Butch gasped, and then Johnny hit him with both hands and he went down. Coolly, Johnny waited for him to get up. And he got up, which made his second mistake. He got up and lunged, head down. A straight left took him over the eyebrow, ripping a gash, and a right uppercut broke his nose. And then Johnny Lyle went to work. What followed was short, interesting, and bloody. When it was over Johnny stood back.

"Now," he said, "get up and pay me sixty dollars for three Slash Seven steers."

"Sixty!" Butch Jensen spluttered. "Steers are going for twelve—fifteen dollars!"

"The steers you butchered are going at twenty dollars," Johnny replied calmly. "If I ever find another hide around here, the price will be thirty dollars."

He turned away, but when he had taken three steps, he stopped. There was a good crowd around, and Johnny was young. This chance was too good to miss.

"You tell Hook Lacey," he said, "that if he ever rustles another head of Slash Seven stock I'll personally come after him!"

Johnny Lyle swaggered just a little as he walked into the Gold Pan and ordered a meal.

Yet as he was eating he began to get red around the

ears. It had been a foolish thing to do, talking like that. Folks would think he was full of hot air.

Then he looked up into a pair of wide blue eyes. "Your order, sir?"

Two days later Chuck Allen rode up to the ranch house and swung down. Bert Ramsey got up hastily from his chair.

"Chuck," he asked eagerly, "you see him?"

Chuck shook his head. "No," he said, "I ain't seen him, but I seen his trail. You better grab yourself a bronc, Bert, and start fogging it for the border. That kid's really started something."

The door opened and Tom West came out. "What's up?" he demanded. His face was gray with worry. "Confound it, what's the matter with these hands? Two days now I've had you all ridin' to find that kid, and you can't turn up a clue! Can't you blind bats even find a tenderfoot kid?"

Chuck grew a little red around the ears, but his eyes twinkled as he looked at Bert out of the corner of his eyes. "I crossed his trail, boss, and she's some trail, believe you me!"

West shoved Bert aside. "Don't stand there like a slab-sided jackass! What happened? Where is he?"

Chuck was taking his time, "Well," he said, "he *was* in Victorio. He rode in there the morning after he left the ranch. He found a couple of Slash Seven hides hanging on Butch Jensen's fence. They'd been burned over into Seven Seventy-sevens, but he found 'em, and then Butch Jensen found him."

"Oh, Lord!" West paled. "If that big brute hurt that kid, I'll kill him!"

"You won't need no war paint," Chuck said, aggravatingly slow, "because the kid took Butch to a swell three-sided whipping. Folks say Johnny just lit all over him, swinging in every direction. He whipped Butch to a frazzle!"

"Chuck," Bert burst out, "you're crazy! Why, that kid couldn't whip one side of—"

"But he did," Chuck interrupted. "He not only beat Butch up, but he made him pay for three head at twenty dollars a head. He further told him that the next hide he found on Butch's fence would cost him thirty dollars."

West swallowed. "And Butch took it?"

"Boss, if you'd seen Butch you'd not ask that question. Butch took everything the kid could throw, which was plenty. Butch looks like he'd crawled facefirst into a den of wildcats. But that ain't all."

They waited, staring at Chuck. He rolled a smoke, taking his time.

"He told everybody who was listening," he finally said, "and probably three or four of 'em was friends of Lacey, that if Hook rustled one more head of our stock, he was going to attend to him personal."

West groaned and Bert Ramsey swallowed. But Chuck was not through.

"Then the kid goes into the Gold Pan. He ain't there more'n thirty minutes before he has that little blond peacherino crazy about him. Mary, she's so crazy about that kid she can't even get her orders straight."

"Chuck," West demanded, "where's Johnny now? If you know, tell me!"

Chuck Allen grew sober. "That's the trouble, boss. I don't know. But when he left Victorio he headed back into the mountains. And that was yesterday afternoon."

Bert Ramsey's face was pale. He liked his job on the Slash Seven and knew West was quite capable of firing him as he had promised. Moreover, he was genuinely worried. That he had considered the boss's nephew a nuisance was true, but anybody who could whip Butch Jensen, and who could collect for stolen cattle, was no tenderfoot, but a man to ride the river with. But to ride into the hills after Hook Lacey, after whipping Jensen, threatening Hook, and then walking off with the girl Hook wanted—that was insanity.

Whipping Jensen was something, but Hook Lacey wouldn't use his fists. He would use a gun, and he had killed seven men, at least. And he would have plenty of help.

West straightened. "Bert," he said harshly, "you get Gar Mullins, Monty Reagan, and Bucky McCann and ride after that kid. And don't come back without him!"

Ramsey nodded. "Yes, sir," he said. "I sure will get him."

"How about me?" Chuck asked. "Can I go, too?"

At the very hour the little cavalcade was leaving the ranch, Johnny Lyle was lying on a ridge looking down into the upper part of the Tierra Blanca Canyon. A thin trail of smoke was lifting from the canyon, and he could see approximately where the camp was. He lay high on the rugged side of Seven Brothers Mountain, with the camp almost fifteen hundred feet below.

"All right, boy," he told himself, "you've made your brags. Now what are you going to do?"

North of the camp the canyon ran due north and south, but just below it took a sharp bend to the west, although a minor canyon trailed off south for a short distance in less rugged country. Their hideout, Johnny could see, was well chosen. There was obviously a spring, judging from the way their camp was located and the looks of the trees and brush, and there was a way out up the canyon to the north.

On the south, they could swing west around the bend. Johnny could see that this trail branched, and the branch beyond also branched. In taking any route they were well covered, with plenty of chance of a getaway unseen, or for defense if they so desired.

•   •   •

Yet if they had to ride north up the canyon there was no way out for several miles. With a posse closing in from the south, one man could stop their escape to the north. Their camp at the spring, however, was so situated that it was nearly impossible for them to be stopped from going south by anything less than a large posse. It was fairly obvious, though, that if they were attacked they would ride south.

The idea that came to him was the wildest kind of a gamble, but he decided to take the chance, for there was a possibility that it might work. To plan ahead was impossible. All he could do was start the ball rolling and take advantage of what opportunity offered.

Mounting his horse, he rode along a bench of Seven Brothers and descended the mountain on the southwest. In the canyon to the west he hastily gathered sticks and built a fire, laying a foundation of crossed dry sticks of some size, gathered from canyon driftwood and arranged in such a way as to burn for some time. The fire was built among rocks and on dry sand so there was no way for it to spread, and no way for it to be seen, though the rising smoke would be visible.

Circling farther south and east, he built three more fires. His hope was that the smoke from all of them would be seen by the outlaws, who would deduce that a posse, having approached during the night, now was preparing breakfast, with every way out blocked. If they decided this, and without a careful scouting expedition, which would consume time, the outlaws would surely retreat up the canyon to the north.

Johnny Lyle worked fast and he worked hard, adding a few sticks of green wood to increase the smoke. When his last fire had been built, he mounted again and rode north on the east side of Stoner Mountain. Now the mountain was between him and the outlaws and he had no idea of what they would do. His gamble was that by riding north, he could hit the canyon of the Tierra Blanca after it swung east, and intercept the escaping outlaws.

He rode swiftly, aware that he could travel faster than they, but with no idea whether or not they had seen his fires and were moving. His first idea was to ride into the bottom of the canyon and meet them face-to-face, but Hook Lacey was a rugged character, as were his men, and the chances were they would elect to fight. He chose the safer way and crawled down among some rocks.

An hour had passed before they appeared. He knew none of them, but rightly guessed the swarthy man with the hook nose was Lacey. He let them get within thirty yards, then yelled:

"All right, boys! Drop your guns and get your hands up! We've got you bottled!"

There was an instant of frozen silence, then Lacey's gun leaped to his hand. He let out a wild yell and the riders charged right up the slope and at Johnny Lyle.

Suddenly panic-stricken, Johnny got off a quick shot that burned the hindquarters of Lacey's plunging horse and hit the pommel of the rider following him. Glancing off, it ripped the following man's arm. Then the riders were right at him.

Johnny sprang aside, working the lever of his Winchester, but they were too close. Wildly he grabbed iron, and then took a wicked blow on the skull from a clubbed six-shooter. He went down, stunned but not out, and managed a quick shot with his six-gun that dropped a man. And then he was up and running. He had only time to grab his Winchester and dive into the rocks.

Cut off from his horse, he was in desperate straits. It would be a matter of minutes, or even seconds, before they would realize only one man had been shooting. Then they would come back.

Scrambling into the rocks, he worked himself higher, striving for a vantage point. They had seen him, though, and a rifle bullet ricocheted off the rocks and whined nastily past his ear. He levered three fast shots from his rifle at the scattering riders. Then the area before him was deserted, the morning warm and still, and the air was empty.

His head throbbed, and when he put a hand to his skull he found that despite his protecting hat, his scalp had been split. Only the fact that the rider had been going away when he fired, and that the felt hat he was wearing was heavy, had saved him from a broken skull.

A sudden move brought a twinge. Looking down, he saw blood on the side of his shirt. Opening it, he saw that a bullet—from where he had no idea—had broken the skin along his side.

Hunkered down behind some rocks, he looked around. His position was fairly secure, though they could approach him from in front and on the right. His field of fire to the front was good, but if they ever got on the cliff across the canyon, he was finished.

What lay behind him he did not know, but the path he had taken along a ledge seemed to dwindle out on the cliff face. He had ammunition, but no water, and no food.

Tentatively he edged along, as if to move forward. A rifle shot splashed splinters in his face and he jerked back, stung.

"Boy," he said to himself, "you've played hob!"

Suddenly he saw a man race across the open in front of him and he fired a belated shot that did nothing but hurry the man. Obviously that man was heading for the cliff across the canyon. Johnny Lyle reloaded his Winchester and checked his pistol. With both loaded he was all set, and he looked behind him at the path. Then he crawled back. As he had suspected, the path dwindled out and there was no escape.

The only way out was among the boulders to his right, from where without doubt the outlaws were also approaching. His rifle ready, he crouched, waiting. Then he came up with a lunge and darted for the nearest boulders. A bullet whipped by his ear, another ricocheted from a rock behind him. Then he hit the sand sliding and scrambled at once to a second boulder.

Someone moved ahead of him, and raising himself to his knees, Johnny shucked his pistol and snapped a quick shot.

There was a brief silence, then a sudden yell and a sound of horses. Instantly there was another shout and a sound of running. Warily Johnny looked out. A stream of riders was rushing up the canyon and the outlaws were riding back down the canyon at breakneck speed.

Carefully, he got to his feet. Gar Mullins was first to see him and he yelled. The others slid to a halt. Limping a little on a bruised leg, Johnny walked toward the horsemen.

"Man," he said, "am I ever glad to see you fellers!"

Ramsey stared at him, sick with relief. "What got into you?" he demanded gruffly. "Trying to tackle that bunch by your lonesome?"

Johnny Lyle explained his fires and the idea he'd had. "Only trouble was," he said ruefully, "they rushed me instead of dropping their guns, but it might've worked!"

Gar Mullins bit off a chew and glanced at Chuck with twinkling eyes. "Had it been me, it would've worked, kid." He glanced at Bert. "Reckon we should finish it now they're on the run?"

"We better let well enough alone," Ramsey said. "If they think there's a posse down canyon, they'll hole up and make a scrap of it. We'd have to dig 'em out one by one."

"I'd rather wait and get 'em in the open," Monty Reagan said honestly. "That Lacey's no bargain." He looked with real respect at Lyle. "Johnny, I take my hat off to you. You got more nerve than me, to tackle that crowd single-handed."

Bucky McCann came up. "He got one, too," he said, gloating. "Pete Gabor's over there with a shot through the head."

"That was luck," Johnny said. "They come right at me and I just cut loose."

"Get any others?"

"Winged one, but it was a ricochet."

Gar spat. "They count," he said, chuckling a little. "We better get out of here."

Considerably chastened, Johnny Lyle fell in alongside of Gar and they started back. Several miles farther along, when they were riding through Sibley Gap, Gar said:

"Old Tom was fit to be tied, kid. You shouldn't ought to go off like that."

"Aw," Johnny protested, "everybody was treating me like a goose-headed tenderfoot! I got tired of it."

The week moved along slowly. Johnny Lyle's head stopped aching and his side began to heal. He rode out to the bog camp every day and worked hard. He was, Ramsey admitted, "a hand." Nothing more was said about his brush with the Lacey gang except for a brief comment by Bucky McCann.

There was talk of a large band of Mexican bandits raiding over the border.

"Shucks," Bucky said carelessly, "nothing to worry about! If they get too rambunctious we'll sic Johnny at 'em! That'll learn 'em!"

But Johnny Lyle was no longer merely the boss's nephew. He was a hand, and he was treated with respect, and given rough friendship.

Nothing more was heard of Lacey. The story had gone around, losing nothing in the telling. The hands of the Slash Seven cow crowd found the story too good to keep. A kid from the Slash Seven, they said, had run Lacey all over the rocks, Lacey and all of his outfit.

Hook Lacey heard the story and flushed with anger. When he thought of the flight of his gang up the canyon from a lot of untended fires, and then their meeting with the Lyle kid, who single-handed not only had stood them off but had killed one man and wounded another, his face burned. If there was one thing he vowed to do, it was to get Johnny Lyle.

Nobody had any actual evidence on Lacey. He was a known rustler, but it had not been proved. Consequently, Lacey showed up around Victorio whenever he was in the mood. And he seemed to be in the mood a great deal after the scrap in Tierra Blanca Canyon. The payoff came suddenly and unexpectedly.

Gar Mullins had orders to ride to Victorio and check to see if a shipment of ammunition and equipment intended for the Slash Seven had arrived. Monty Reagan was to go along, but Monty didn't return from the bog camp in time, so Lyle asked his uncle if he could go.

Reluctantly, Tom West told him to go ahead. "But don't you go asking for trouble!" he said irritably. But in his voice was an underlying note of pride, too. After all, he admitted, the kid came of fighting stock. "If anybody braces you, that's different!"

Victorio was basking in a warm morning sun when the two cowhands rode into the street. Tying up at the Gold Pan, Johnny left Gar to check on the supplies while he went to get a piece of apple pie. Not that he was fooling Gar, or even himself. It was that blonde behind the counter that he wanted to see.

Hook Lacey was drinking coffee when Johnny entered. Lacey looked up, then set his cup down hard, almost spilling the coffee.

Mary smiled quickly at Johnny, then threw a frightened look at Lacey.

"Hello, Johnny," she said, her voice almost failing her. "I—I didn't expect you."

Johnny was wary. He had recognized Lacey at once, but his uncle had said he wasn't to look for trouble.

"Got any apple pie?" he asked.

She placed a thick piece before him, then filled a cup with coffee. Johnny grinned at her and began to eat. "Mmm!" he said, liking the pie. "You make this?"

"No, my mother did."

"She sure makes good pie!" Johnny was enthusiastic. "I've got to get over here more often!"

"Surprised they let you get away from home," Lacey said, "but I see you brought a nursemaid with you."

Now, Tom West had advised Johnny to keep out of trouble, and Johnny, an engaging and easygoing fellow, intended to do just that, up to a point. This was the point.

"I didn't need a nursemaid over on the Tierra Blanca," he said cheerfully. "From the way you hightailed over them rocks, I figured it was you needed one!"

Lacey's face flamed. He came off the bench, his face dark with anger. "Why, you—"

Johnny looked around at him. "Better not start anything," he said. "You ain't got a gang with you."

Lacey was in a quandary. Obviously the girl was more friendly to Johnny than to him. That meant that he could expect no help from her should she be called on to give testimony following a killing. If he drew first he was a gone gosling, for he knew enough about old Tom West to know the Slash Seven outfit would never stop hunting if this kid was killed in anything but a fair fight. And the kid wasn't even on his feet.

"Listen!" he said harshly. "You get out of town! If you're in this town one hour from now, I'll kill you!"

Slamming down a coin on the counter, he strode from the restaurant.

"Oh, Johnny!" Mary's face was white and frightened. "Don't stay here! Go now! I'll tell Gar where you are. Please go!"

"Go?" Johnny was feeling a fluttering in his stomach, but it angered him that Mary should feel he had to leave. "I will not go! I'll run *him* out of town!"

Despite her pleading, he turned to the door and walked outside. Gar Mullins was nowhere in sight. Neither was Lacey. But a tall, stooped man with his arm in a sling stood across the street, and Johnny Lyle guessed at once that he was a lookout, that here was the man he had winged in the canyon fight. And winged though the man was, it was his left arm, and his gun hung under his right hand.

Johnny Lyle hesitated. Cool common sense told him that it would be better to leave. Actually, Uncle Tom and the boys all knew he had nerve enough, and it was no cowardice to dodge a shoot-out with a killer like Hook Lacey. The boys had agreed they wouldn't want to tangle with him.

Just the same, Johnny doubted that any one of them would dodge a scrap if it came to that. And all his Texas blood and training rebelled against the idea of being run out of town. Besides, there was Mary. It would look like he was a pure D coward to run out now.

Yet what was the alternative? Within an hour, Hook Lacey would come hunting him. Hook would choose the ground, place, and time of meeting. And Hook was no fool. He knew all the tricks.

What, then, to do?

The only thing, Johnny Lyle decided, was to meet Lacey first. To hunt the outlaw down and force him into a fight before he was ready. There was nothing wrong with using strategy, with using a trick. Many gunfighters had done it. Billy the Kid had done it against the would-be killer, Joe Grant. Wes Hardin had used many a device.

Yet what to do? And where? Johnny Lyle turned toward the corral with a sudden idea in mind. Suppose he could appear to have left town? Wouldn't that lookout go to Hook with the news? Then he could come back, ease up to Lacey suddenly, and call him, then draw.

Gar Mullins saw Johnny walking toward the corral, then he spotted the lookout. Mullins intercepted Johnny just as he stepped into saddle.

"What's up, kid? You in trouble?"

Briefly Johnny explained. Gar listened and, much to

Johnny's relief, registered no protest. "All right, kid. You got it to do if you stay in this country, and your idea's a good one. You ever been in a shoot-out before?"

"No, I sure haven't."

"Now, look. You draw natural, see? Don't pay no mind to being faster'n he is. Chances are you ain't anywheres close to that. You figure on getting that first shot right where it matters, you hear? Shoot him in the body, right in the middle. No matter what happens, hit him with the first shot, you hear me?"

"Yeah."

Johnny felt sick at his stomach and his mouth was dry, his heart pounding.

"I'll handle that lookout, so don't pay him no mind." Gar looked up. "You a good shot, Johnny?"

"On a target I can put five shots in a playing card."

"That's all right, but this card'll be shooting back. But don't you worry. You choose your own spot for it."

"Wait!" Johnny had an idea. "Listen, you have somebody get word to him that Butch Jensen wants to see him. I'll be across the street at the wagon yard. When he comes up, I'll step out."

He rode swiftly out of town. Glancing back, he saw the lookout watching. Gar Mullins put a pack behind his own saddle and apparently readied his horse for the trail. Then he walked back down the street.

He was just opposite the wagon yard when he saw the lookout stop on a street corner, looking at him. At the same instant, Hook Lacey stepped from behind a wagon. Across the street was Webb Foster, another of the Lacey crowd. There was no mistaking their purpose, and they had him boxed!

Gar Mullins was thirty-eight, accounted an old man on the frontier, and he had seen and taken part in some wicked gun battles. Yet now he saw his position clearly.

This was it, and he wasn't going to get out of this one. If Johnny had been with him—but Johnny wouldn't be in position for another ten minutes.

Hook Lacey was smiling. "You were in the canyon the other day, Gar," he said triumphantly. "Now you'll see what it's like. We're going to kill you, Gar. Then we'll follow that kid and get him. You ain't got a chance, Gar."

Mullins knew it, yet with a little time, even a minute, he might have.

"Plannin' on wiping out the Slash Seven, Hook?" he drawled. "That's what you'll have to do if you kill that kid. He's the old man's nephew."

"Ain't you worried about yourself, Gar?" Lacey sneered. "Or are you just wet-nursing that kid?"

Gar's seamed and hard face was set. His eyes flickered to the lookout, whose hand hovered only an inch above his gun. And to Webb, with his thumb hooked in his belt. There was no use waiting. It would be minutes before the kid would be set.

And then the kid's voice sounded, sharp and clear.

"I'll take Lacey, Gar! *Get that lookout!*"

Hook Lacey whipped around, drawing as he turned. Johnny Lyle, who had left his horse and hurried right back, grabbed for his gun. He saw the big, hard-faced man before him, saw him clear and sharp. Saw his hand flashing down, saw the broken button on his shirtfront, saw the Bull Durham tag from his pocket, saw the big gun come up. But his own gun was rising, too.

The sudden voice, the turn, all conspired to throw Lacey off, yet he had drawn fast and it was with shock that he saw the kid's gun was only a breath slower. It was that which got him, for he saw that gun rising and he shot too quick. The bullet tugged at Johnny's shirt collar, and then Johnny, with that broken button before his eyes, fired.

Two shots, with a tiny but definite space between them, and then Johnny looked past Lacey at the gun exploding in Webb Foster's hands. He fired just as Gar Mullins swung his gun to Webb. Foster's shot glanced off the iron rim of a wagon wheel just as Gar's bullet crossed Johnny's in Webb Foster's body.

The outlaw crumpled slowly, grabbed at the porch awning, then fell off into the street.

Johnny stood very still. His eyes went to the lookout, who was on his hands and knees on the ground, blood dripping in great splashes from his body. Then they went to Hook Lacey. The broken button was gone, and there was an edge cut from the tobacco tag. Hook Lacey was through, his chips all cashed. He had stolen his last horse.

Gar Mullins looked at Johnny Lyle and grinned weakly. "Kid," he said softly, walking toward him, hand outstretched, "we make a team. Here on out, it's saddle partners, hey?"

"Sure, Gar." Johnny did not look again at Lacey. He looked into the once bleak blue eyes of Mullins. "I ride better with a partner. You got that stuff for the ranch?"

"Yeah."

"Then if you'll pick up my horse in the willows, yonder, I'll say good-bye to Mary. We'd best be getting back. Uncle Tom'll be worried."

Gar Mullins chuckled, walking across the street, arm in arm with Johnny.

"Well, he needn't be," Gar said. "He needn't be."

In Victorio's
Country

The four riders, hard-bitten men bred to the desert and the gun, pushed steadily southward. "Red" Clanahan, a monstrous big man with a wide-jawed bulldog face and a thick neck descending into massive shoulders, held the lead. Behind him, usually in single file but occasionally bunching, trailed the others.

It was hot and still. The desert of southern Arizona's Apache country was rarely pleasant in the summer, and this day was no exception. "Bronco" Smith, who trailed just behind Red, mopped his lean face with a handkerchief and cursed fluently, if monotonously.

He had his nickname from the original meaning of the term *wild and unruly* and the Smith was a mere convenience, in respect to the custom that insists a man have two names. The "Dutchman" defied the rule by having none at all, or if he had once owned a name, it was probably recorded only upon some forgotten reward poster lining the bottom of some remote sheriff's desk drawer. To the southwestern desert country he was simply and sufficiently, the Dutchman.

As for "Yaqui Joe," he was called just that, or was referred to as the "breed" and everyone knew without question who was indicated. He was a wide-faced man with a square jaw, stolid and silent, a man of varied frontier skills, but destined to follow always where another led. A man who had known much hardship and no kindness, but whose commanding virtue was loyalty.

Smith was a lean whip of a man with slightly graying hair, stooped shoulders, and spidery legs. Dried and parched by desert winds, he was as tough as cowhide and iron. It was said that he had shot his way out of more places than most men had ever walked into, and he would have followed no man's leadership but that of Big Red Clanahan.

The Dutchman was a distinct contrast to the lean frame of Smith, for he was fat, and not in the stomach alone, but all over his square, thick-boned body. Yet the blue eyes that stared from his round cheeks were sleepy, wise, and wary.

There were those who said that Yaqui Joe's father had been an Irishman, but his name was taken from his mother in the mountains of Sonora. He had been an outlaw by nature and choice from the time he could crawl, and he was minus a finger on his left hand, and had a notch in the top of his ear. The bullet that had so narrowly missed his skull had been fired by a man who never missed again. He was buried in a hasty grave somewhere in the Mogollons.

Of them all, Joe was the only one who might have been considered a true outlaw. All had grown up in a land and time when the line was hard to draw.

Big Red had never examined his place in society. He did not look upon himself as a thief or as a criminal, and would have been indignant to the point of shooting had anybody suggested he was either of these. However, the fact was that Big Red had long since strayed over the border that divides the merely careless from the actually criminal. Like many another westerner he had branded unbranded cattle on the range, as in the years following the War Between the States the cattle were there for the first comer who possessed a rope and a hot iron.

It was a business that kept him reasonably well supplied with poker and whiskey money, but when all available cattle wore brands, it seemed to him the difference in branded and unbranded cattle was largely a matter of time. All the cattle had been mavericks after the war, and if a herd wore a brand it simply meant the cattleman had reached them before he did. "Big Red" accepted this as a mere detail, and a situation that could be speedily rectified with a cinch ring, and in this he was not alone.

If the cattleman who preceded him objected with lead, Clanahan accepted this as an occupational hazard.

However, from rustling cattle to taking the money itself was a short step, and halved the time consumed in branding and selling the cattle. Somewhere along this trail Big Red crossed, all unwittingly at the time, the shadow line that divides the merely careless from the actually dishonest, and at about the time he crossed this line, Big Red separated from the man who had ridden beside him for five long, hard frontier years.

The young hardcase who had punched cows and ridden the trail herds to Kansas at his side was equally big and equally Irish, and his name was Bill Gleason.

When Clanahan took to the outlaw trail, Gleason turned to the law. Neither took the direction he followed with any intent. It was simply that Clanahan failed to draw a line that Gleason drew, and that Gleason, being a skillful man on a trail, and a fast hand with a gun, became the sheriff of the country that held his home town of Cholla.

The trail of Big Red swung as wide as his loop, and he covered a lot of country. Being the man he was, he soon won to the top of his profession, if such it might be called. And this brought about a situation.

Cholla had a bank. As there were several big ranchers in the area, and two well-paying gold mines, the bank was solvent, extremely so. It was fairly, rumor said, bulging with gold. This situation naturally attracted attention.

Along the border that divides Mexico from Arizona, New Mexico, and Texas was an ambitious and overly bloodthirsty young outlaw known as Ramon Zappe. Cholla and its bank intrigued him, and as his success had been striking and even brilliant, he rode down upon the town of Cholla with confidence and seven riders.

Dismounting in front of the bank, four of the men went inside, one of them being Zappe himself. The other four, with rifles ready, waited for the town to react, but nothing happened. Zappe held this as due to his own reputation, and strutted accordingly.

The bank money was passed over by silent and efficient tellers, the bandits remounted, and in leisurely fashion began to depart. And then something happened that was not included in their plans. It was something that created an impression wherever bad men were wont to gather.

From behind a stone wall on the edge of town came a withering blast of fire, and in the space of no more than fifty yards, five of the bandits died. Two more were hung to a convenient cottonwood on the edge of town. Only one man, mounted upon an exceptionally fast horse, escaped.

Along the dim trails this was put down to chance, but one man dissented, and that man was Big Red Clanahan, for Big Red had not forgotten the hard-bitten young rider who had accompanied him upon so many long trails, and who had stood beside him to cow a Dodge City saloon full of gunfighters. Big Red remembered Bill Gleason, and smiled.

Twice in succeeding months the same thing happened, and they were attended by only one difference. On those two occasions not one man survived. Cholla was distinctly a place to stay away from.

Big Red was intrigued and tantalized. Although he would have been puzzled by the term, Big Red was in his own way an artist. He was also a tactician, and a man with a sense of humor. He met Yaqui Joe in a little town below the border, and over frequent glasses of tequila, he probed the half-breed's mind, searching for the gimmick that made Cholla foolproof against the outlaw raids.

There had to be something, some signal. If he could learn it, he would find it amusing and a good joke on Bill to drop in, rob Cholla's bank, and get away, thumbing his nose at his old pard.

The time was good. Victorio was on the warpath and had run off horses from the army, killed some soldiers, and fought several pitched battles in which he had come off well, if not always the victor. The country was restless and frightened and pursuit would neither be easily organized nor long continued when every man was afraid to be long away from home.

"Think!" Red struck his hairy fist on the table between them. "Think, Joe! There has to be a signal! Those hombres didn't just pop out of the ground!"

Yaqui Joe shook his head, staring with bleary eyes into his glass. "I remember nothing—nothing. Except . . ."

His voice trailed off, but Big Red grabbed his shoulder and shook him.

"Except what, Joe? Somethin' that was different! *Think!*"

Yaqui Joe scowled in an effort to round up his thoughts and get a rope on the idea that had come to him. They had been over this so many times before.

"There was nothing!" he insisted. "Only, while we sat in front of the bank, there was a sort of light, like from a glass and the sun. It moved quickly across the street. Like so!" He gestured widely with his hand, knocking his glass to the floor.

Clanahan picked up the glass and filled it once more. He was scowling.

"And that was all? Yuh're shore?"

Waiting until he was sure Gleason was out of town, Big Red rode in. He did not like to do it, but preferred not to trust to anyone else. At the bank he changed some money, glancing casually around. Then his pulse jumped, and he grinned at the teller who handed him his money.

He walked from the bank, stowing away his money. So that was it! And of course, it could be nothing else.

The bank stood in such a position that the windows caught the full glare of the morning light, and that sunlight flowed through the windows and fell full upon the mirror that covered the upper half of the door that led behind the wickets where the money was kept.

If that door was opened suddenly, a flash of light would be thrown into the windows across the street! A flash that would run along the storefronts the length of the street, throwing the glare into the eyes of the bartender in the saloon, the grocer and the hardware man, and ending upon the faces of the loafers before the livery stable. One at least, and probably more, would see that flash, and the warning would have been given.

He gathered his men carefully, and he knew the men to get for the job. Yaqui Joe, because when sober he was one lump of cold nerve, then Bronco Smith and the Dutchman because they were new in the Cholla country, and skillful, able workmen. Then he waited until Victorio was raiding in the vicinity, and sent a startled Mexican into town with news of the Apache.

With Sheriff Bill Gleason in command, over half the able-bodied men rode out of town, and Big Red, with Yaqui Joe at his side, rode in. Bronco Smith and the Dutchman had come in a few minutes earlier, and it was Smith who blocked the opening of the mirrored door.

The job was swift and smooth. The three men in the bank, taken aback by the blocking of their signal, were tied hand and foot and the money loaded into canvas bags. The four were on their way out of town before a sitter in front of the livery stable recognized the half-breed.

Under a hot, metallic sky the desert lay like a crumpled sheet of dusty copper, scattered with occasional boulders. Here and there it was tufted with cactuses or Joshua palm and slashed by the cancerous scars of dry washes. A lone ranch six miles south of Cholla fell behind them and they pushed on into the afternoon, riding not swiftly but steadily.

Clanahan turned in the saddle and glanced back. His big jaws moved easily over the cud of chewing tobacco, his gray-green eyes squinting against the hard bright glare of the sun.

"Anything in sight?" Bronco did not look around. "Mebbe we'll lose 'em quick."

"Gleason ain't easy lost."

"You got respect for that sheriff."

"I know him."

"Maybe Joe's idea goot one, no?" The Dutchman struck a match with his left hand cupping it to his cigarette with his palm. "Maybe in Apache country they will not follow?"

"They'll follow. Only in Victorio's country they may not follow far. When we shift hosses we'll be all set."

"How far to the hosses?"

"Only a few miles." Red indicated a saw-toothed ridge on the horizon. "Yonder."

"We got plenty moneys, no?" The Dutchman slapped a thick palm on his saddlebags and was rewarded with the chink of gold coin. "Och! Mexico City! We go there and I show you how a gentlemans shall live! Mexico City with money to spend! There iss nothing better!"

Two ridges gaped at the sky when they reached the horses, two ridges that lay open like the jaws of a skull. Red Clanahan turned his horse from the dim trail he had

followed and dipped down into the gap where lay a wide
space of flat ground, partially shaded by two upthrust
ledges that held a forty-degree angle above the ground.
Four horses waited there, and two pack mules.

Smith nodded, satisfied. "Those mules will take the
weight of the gold off our hosses. Grub, too! Yuh think of
everything, Red!"

"There's a spring under that corner rock. Better
dump yore canteens and refill them. Don't waste any
time."

"How about south of here?" Bronco stared off over
the desert. "Is there more water?"

"Plenty water." Joe accepted the question. "Latigo
Springs tomorrow night, and the day after Seepin'
Springs."

"Good!" Smith bit off a chew of his own. "I was dry
as a ten-year-old burro bone when I got here."

He needed nobody to tell him what that bleak waste
to the south would be like without water, or how difficult
to find water it would be unless you knew where to look.

"How much did we get?" Dutch inquired. "How
much? You know, eh?"

"Fifty thousand, or about."

"I'd settle for half!" Smith spat.

"Yuh'll settle for a lot less." Red turned his hard
green eyes on Smith. "I'm takin' the top off this one. Took
me four weeks of playin' tag with Gleason to get the lay-
out."

"What do yuh call the top?"

"Seventeen thousand, if she comes to fifty. You get
eleven thousand apiece."

Bronco pondered the thought. It was enough. In
seven years of outlawry he had never had more than five
hundred dollars at one time. Anyway, he wouldn't have
stayed that close to Gleason for twice the money. That
sheriff had a nose for trouble.

When Big Red first suggested the raid on Cholla,
Smith had thought him crazy, but he had to chuckle when

he remembered the astonishment on the cashier's face when he stepped around and blocked the door with the mirror before it could be opened, and how "Big Red" had come in through the door on the other side that looked like it wasn't there.

The escape into Victorio's country was pure genius—if they avoided the Apaches. Yaqui Joe's idea had been a good one, but Red had already planned it in advance, as was proved by the waiting horses. Of necessity a pursuing force would have to go slow to avoid the Indians, and they would have no fresh horses awaiting them at the notch.

Under a hot and brassy sky they held steadily southward over a strange, wild land of tawny yellows and reds, bordered by serrated ridges that gnawed at the sky. Clanahan mopped the sweat from his brow and stared back over the trail, lost in dancing heat waves. As usual there was nothing in sight.

Hours passed, and the only movement aside from the walking of their horses was the wavering heat vibrations and, high under the sun-filled dome of the sky, the distant black circling of a buzzard. On the ground not even a horned frog or a Gila monster showed under the withering sun.

"How much farther to water, Joe?"

"One, maybe two mile."

"We'll drink and refill our canteens," Red told them, "but we stop no longer than that. We've got gold enough to do somethin' with and we'd better be gettin' on."

"No sign of 'Paches."

Red shrugged, then spat, wiping the sweat from the inside of his hatband.

"The time to look for Injuns is when there's no sign. Yuh can bet the desert's alive with 'em, but if we're lucky they won't see us."

Latigo Spring was a round pool of milky-blue water

supplied by a thin trickle from a crack in the sandrock that shaded it. The trickle waged a desperate war with the sun's heat and the thirsty earth. Occasionally, it held its own, but now in the late summer, the water was low.

They swung down and drank, then they held their canteens into the thin flow of the spring. They filled slowly. One by one they sponged out the nostrils and mouths of their horses and led the grateful animals to the water.

Bronco wandered out to where he could look back over their trail. He shaded his eyes against the sun, but then as he started to turn back, he hesitated, staring at the ground.

"Red." His voice was normal in tone, but it rang loudly in the clear, empty air.

Caught by some meaningful timbre in his tone, the others looked up. They were wary men, alert for danger and expecting it. They knew the chance they took, crossing Victorio's country at this time, and trouble could blossom from the most barren earth.

Big Red slouched over on the run-down heels of his worn boots. Mopping his face and neck with a bandanna, he stared at the tracks Bronco indicated.

Two horses had stood here. Two riders had dismounted, but not for long.

"Hey!" Clanahan squatted on his heels. "Those are kids' tracks!"

"Uh-huh." Bronco swore softly. "Kids! Runnin' loose in Apache country. Where yuh reckon they came from, Red?"

Red squinted off to the south and west. The direction of the tracks was but little west of their own route.

"What I'm wonderin' is where they are goin'," he said dubiously. "They shore ain't headed for nowhere, thataway, and right smack into the dead center of the worst Injun country!"

Smith stared off over the desert, shook his head wonderingly, then walked back to the spring and drank deeply once more. He was a typical man of the trail. He drank when there was water, ate whenever there was food, rested whenever there was a moment to relax, well knowing days might come when none of the three could be had. He straightened then, wiping the stubble of beard around his mouth with the back of his hand.

"Somet'ing iss wrong?" The Dutchman glanced at Red. "What iss, aboot a kid?"

"Couple of youngsters ridin' south. Boy, mebbe thirteen or fourteen, and a girl about the same age." He mopped his face again, and replaced his hat. "Mount up."

They swung into their saddles and Red shifted his bulk to an easy seat. The saddle had grown uncomfortably hot in the brief halt. They started on, walking their horses. It was easy to kill a good horse in this heat. Suddenly the trail the kids were taking veered sharply west. Clanahan reined in and stared at it.

"Childer!" The Dutchman exclaimed in a puzzled voice. "Und vhy here?"

"They are shore headin' into trouble," Smith said, staring at their trail. His eyes stole sheepishly toward Clanahan, and he started to speak, then held his peace.

The Dutchman sat stolidly in the saddle. "Mine sister," he said suddenly, absently, "has two childer. Goot poys."

Yaqui Joe looked over his shoulder at their trail, but it was empty and still. Off on their far right a line of magenta-colored ridges seemed to be stretching long fingers of stone toward the trail the kids had taken, as though to intercept them. A tuft of cactus lifted from the crest of the nearest hill like the hackles on an angry dog.

Red's mouth was dry and he dug into his shirt pocket for his plug and bit off a sizable chunk. He rolled it in his big jaws and started his horse moving along the trail to the west, following the two weary horses the youngsters were riding.

171

Smith stared at the desert. "Glory, but it's hot!"

He suddenly knew he was relieved. He had been afraid Red would want to hold to their own route. Safety lay south, only danger and death could await them in the west, but he kept thinking of those kids, and remembering what Apaches could do to a person before that person was lucky enough to die. Thoughtfully, he slipped a shell from a belt loop and dropped it into his shirt pocket.

An hour had passed before Clanahan halted again, and then he lifted a hand.

"Joe," he said, "come up here."

The four gathered in a grim, sun-beaten line. Five unshod ponies had come in from the east and were following the trail the youngsters had left.

"'Paches," Joe said. "Five of them."

Red's horse seemed to start moving of its own volition, but as it walked forward Red dropped a hand to the stock of his Winchester and slid it out and laid it across his saddlebow. The others did likewise.

Suddenly, with the tracks of those unshod ponies, the desert became a place of stealthy menace. These men had fought Apaches before, and they knew the deadly desert warriors were men to be reckoned with. The horses walked a little faster now, and the eyes of the four men roved unceasingly over the mirage-haunted desert.

Then the faraway boom of a rifle jarred them from their drowsy watchfulness. Red's gelding stretched his long legs into a fast canter toward a long spine of rock that arched its broken vertebrae against the sky. Suddenly he slowed down. The rifle boomed again.

"That's a Henry," Bronco said. "The kid's got him a good rifle."

Red halted where the rocks ended and stood in his stirrups. A puff of smoke lifted from a tiny hillock in the basin beyond, and across the hillock he could see that two horses were down. Dead, or merely lying out of harm's way?

In the foreground he picked up a slight movement as

a slim brown body wormed forward. The other men had dropped from their saddles and moved up. Still standing in his stirrups, Clanahan threw his Winchester to his shoulder, sighted briefly, then fired.

The Apaches leaped, screamed piercingly, then plunged over into a tangle of cholla. Bronco and the Dutchman fired as one man, then Joe fired. An Indian scrambled to his feet and made a break for the shelter of some rocks. Three rifles boomed at once, and the Indian halted abruptly, took two erect, stilted steps, and plunged over on his face.

They rode forward warily, and Clanahan saw a boy, probably fifteen years old, rise from behind the hillock, relief strong in his handsome blue eyes.

"Shore glad to see yuh, mister." His voice steadied. "I reckon they was too many for me."

Red shoved his hat back and spat. "You was doin' all right, boy." His eyes shifted to the girl, a big-eyed, too thin child of thirteen or so. "What in thunderation are yuh doin' in this country? This here's 'Pache country. Don't yuh know that?"

The lad's face reddened. "Reckon we was headed for Pete Kitchen's place, mister. I heerd he was goin' to stay on, Injuns or no, an' we reckoned he might need help."

Clanahan nodded. "Kitchen's stayin' on, all right, and he can use help. He's a good man, Pete is. Your sister work, too?"

"She cooks mighty good, washes dishes, mends." The boy looked up eagerly. "You fellers wouldn't be needin' no help, would yuh? We need work powerful bad. Pa, he got hisself killed over to Mobeetie, and we got our wagon stole."

"Jimmy stole the horses back!" the girl said proudly. "He's mighty brave, Jimmy is! He's my brother!"

Clanahan swallowed. "Reckon he is, little lady. I shore reckon."

"He got him an Injun out there," Smith offered. "Dead center."

"I did?" The boy was excited and proud. "I guess," he added a little self-consciously, "I get to put a notch on my rifle now!"

Bronco started and stared at Red, and the big man hunkered down, the sunlight glinting on his rust-red hair.

"Son, don't yuh put no notch on yore rifle, nor ever on yore gun. That there's a tinhorn trick, and you ain't no tinhorn. Anyway," he added thoughtfully, "I guess killin' a man ain't nothin' to be proud of, not even an Injun. Even when it has to be did."

The Dutchman shifted uneasily, glancing at the back trail. Yaqui Joe, after the manner of his people, was not worried. He squatted on his heels and lighted a cigarette, drowsing in the hot, still afternoon.

"We better be gettin' on," Clanahan said, straightening. "Them shots will be callin' more Injuns. I reckon you two got to get to Kitchen's all right, and this is no country to be travelin' with no girl, no matter how good a shot yuh are. That Victorio's a he-wolf. We better get on."

"Won't do no good, Red," Smith said suddenly. "Here they come!"

"Gleason?"

"No. More 'Paches!"

A shot's flat sound dropped into the stillness and heat, and the ripples of its widening circle of sound echoed from the rocks. Joe hit the ground with his face twisted.

"Got me!" he grunted, staring at the torn flesh of his calf and the crimson of the blood staining his leg and the torn pants.

Clanahan rolled over on his stomach behind a thick clump of creosote bush and shifted his Winchester. The basin echoed with the flat, absentminded reports of the guns. Silence hung heavy in the heat waves for minutes at a time, and then a gun boomed and the stillness was spread apart by a sound that was almost a physical blow.

Sweat trickled into Red's eyes and they smarted bitterly. He dug into his belt loops and laid out a neat row of cartridges. Once, glancing around, Red saw that the little girl was bandaging Joe's leg while the Yaqui stared in puzzled astonishment at her agile, white fingers.

Out on the lip of the basin a brown leg showed briefly against the brown sand. Warned by the movement, Clanahan pointed a finger of lead and the Apache reared up, and the Dutchman's Henry boomed.

It was very hot. A bullet kicked sand into Red's eyes and mouth. His worn shirt smelled of the heat and of stale sweat. He scratched his jaw where it itched and peered down across the little knoll.

Across the basin a rifle sounded, and Smith's body tensed sharply and he gave out a long "Aaahh!" of sound, drawn out and deep. Red turned his head toward his friend and the movement drew three quick shots that showered him with gravel. He rolled over, changing position.

Bronco Smith had taken a bullet through the top of the shoulder as he lay on his stomach in the sand, and it had buried itself deep within him, penetrating a lung, by the look of the froth on his lips.

Smith spat and turned his eyes toward Red. "Anyhow," he said hoarsely, "we put one over on Gleason."

"Yeah."

Red shifted his Winchester, and when an Apache slithered forward, he caught him in the side with a bullet, then shifted his fire again.

Then for a long time nothing seemed to happen. A dust devil danced in from the waste of the desert and beat out its heart in a clump of ironwood. Red turned his head cautiously and looked at the boy. "How's it, son? Hotter'n blazes, ain't it?"

Later, the afternoon seemed to catch a hint from the purple horizon and began to lower its sun more rapidly. The nearby rocks took on a pastel pink that faded, and in the fading light the Apaches gambled on a rush.

Guns from the hollow boomed, and two Indians dropped, and then another. The rest vanished as if by a strong wind, but they were out there waiting. Clanahan shifted his position cautiously, fed shells into his gun, and remembered a black-eyed girl in Juarez.

A lizard, crawling from a rock, its tiny body quivering with heat and the excited beat of its little heart as it stared in mute astonishment at the rust-red head of the big man with the rifle.

Sheriff Bill Gleason drew up. When morning found the posse far into the desert, he decided he would ride forward until noon, and then turn back. The men who rode with him were nervous about their families and homes, and to go farther would lead to out-and-out mutiny. It was now mid-morning, and the tracks still held west.

"Clanahan's crazy!" Eckles, the storekeeper in Cholla, said. He was a talkative man, and had been the last to see and the first to mention that Big Red was on a trail. "What's he headin' west for? His only chance is south!"

Ollie Weedin, one of the Cholla townsmen, nudged Gleason. "Buzzards, Bill. Look!"

"Let's go," Gleason said, feeling something tighten up within him. The four they trailed were curly wolves who had cut their teeth on hot lead, but in the Apache country it was different.

"Serves 'em right if the Injuns got 'em!" Eckles said irritably. "Cussed thieves!"

Weedin glanced at him in distaste. "Better men than you'll ever be, Eckles!"

The storekeeper looked at Weedin, shocked. "Why, they are thieves!" he exclaimed indignantly.

"Shore," someone said, "but sometimes these days the line is hard to draw. They took a wrong turn, somewheres. That Clanahan was a good man with a rope."

In the hollow band of hills where the trail led, they

saw a lone gray gelding, standing drowsily near a clump of mesquite. And then they saw the dark, still forms on the ground as their horses walked forward. No man among them but had seen this before, the payoff where Indian met white man and both trails were washed out in blood and gun smoke.

"They done some shootin'!" Weedin said. "Four Apaches on this side."

"Five," Gleason said. "There's one beyond that clump of greasewood."

A movement brought their guns up, and then they stopped. A slim boy with a shock of corn-colored hair stood silently awaiting them in sun-faded jeans and checkered shirt. Beside him was a knobby-kneed girl who clutched his sleeve.

"We're all that's left, mister," the boy said.

Gleason glanced around. The eyes of Yaqui Joe stared into the bright sun, still astonished at the white fingers that had bandaged his leg in probably the only kindness he had ever experienced. He had been shot twice in the chest, aside from the leg wound.

Bronco Smith lay where he had taken his bullet, the gravel at his mouth dark with stain.

The Dutchman, placid in death as in life, held a single shell in his stiff fingers and the breech of his rifle was open.

Gleason glanced around, but said nothing. He turned at the excited yell from Eckles. "Here's the bank's money! On these dead mules!"

Ollie Weedin stole a glance at the sheriff, but said nothing. Eckles looked around and started to speak, but at Weedin's hard glare he hesitated, and swallowed.

"It was one buster of a fight," somebody said.

"There's seventeen Injuns dead," the boy offered. "None got away."

"When did this fight end, boy?" Gleason asked.

"Last night, about dusk. They was six of 'em first. I got me one, and he got two or three with a six-shooter.

Then they was more come, and a fight kind of close up. I couldn't see, as it was purty dark, but it didn't last long."

Gleason looked at him and chewed his mustache. "Where'd that last fight take place, son?" he asked.

"Yonder."

Silently the men trooped over. There was a lot of blood around and the ground badly ripped up. Both Indians there were dead, one killed with his own knife.

Weedin stole a cautious look around, but the other men looked uncomfortable and, after a moment of hesitation, began to troop back toward their horses. Gleason noticed the boy's eyes shoot a quick, frightened glance toward a clump of brush and rocks, but ignored it.

Ollie shifted his feet.

"Reckon we better get started, Bill? Wouldn't want no running fight with those kids with us."

"Yuh're right. Better mount up."

He hesitated, briefly. The scarred ground held his eyes and he scowled, as if trying to read some message in the marks of the battle. Then he turned and walked toward his horse.

All of them avoided glancing toward the steeldust, and if anyone saw the sheriff's canteen slip from his hand and lie on the sand forgotten, they said nothing.

Eckles glanced once at the horse that dozed by the mesquite, but before he could speak his eyes met Ollie Weedin's and he gulped and looked hastily away. They moved off then, and no man turned to look back. Eckles forced a chuckle.

"Well, kid," he said to the boy, "yuh've killed yuh some Injuns, so I reckon youh'll be carvin' a notch or two on your rifle now."

The boy shook his head stiffly. "Not me," he said scornfully. "That's a tinhorn's trick!"

Gleason looked over at Ollie and smiled. "Yuh got a chaw, Ollie?"

"Shore haven't, Bill. Reckon I must have lost mine, back yonder."

ABOUT LOUIS
L'AMOUR

"I think of myself in the oral tradition—as a troubadour, a village tale-teller, the man in the shadows of the campfire. That's the way I'd like to be remembered—as a storyteller. A good storyteller."

It is doubtful that any author could be as at home in the world re-created in his novels as Louis Dearborn L'Amour. Not only could he physically fill the boots of the rugged characters he wrote about, but he literally "walked the land my characters walk." His personal experiences as well as his lifelong devotion to historical research combined to give Mr. L'Amour the unique knowledge and understanding of people, events, and the challenge of the American frontier that became the hallmarks of his popularity.

Of French-Irish descent, Mr. L'Amour could trace his own family in North America back to the early 1600s and follow their steady progression westward, "always on the frontier." As a boy growing up in Jamestown, North Dakota, he absorbed all he could about his family's frontier heritage, including the story of his great-grandfather who was scalped by Sioux warriors.

Spurred by an eager curiosity and desire to broaden his horizons, Mr. L'Amour left home at the age of fifteen and enjoyed a wide variety of jobs including seaman, lumberjack, elephant handler, skinner of dead cattle, assessment miner, and an officer in the tank destroyers during World War II. During his "yondering" days he also circled the world on a freighter, sailed a dhow on the Red Sea, was shipwrecked in the West Indies and stranded in the Mojave Desert. He won fifty-one of fifty-nine fights as a professional boxer and worked as a journalist and lecturer. He was a voracious reader and collector of rare books. His personal library contained 17,000 volumes.

Mr. L'Amour "wanted to write almost from the time I could talk." After developing a widespread following for his many frontier and adventure stories written for fiction magazines, Mr. L'Amour published his first full-length novel, *Hondo,* in the United States in 1953. Every one of his more than 100 books is in print; there are nearly 230 million copies of his books in print worldwide, making him one of the bestselling authors in modern literary history. His books have been translated into twenty languages, and more than forty-five of his novels and stories have been made into feature films and television movies.

His hardcover bestsellers include *The Lonesome Gods, The Walking Drum* (his twelfth-century historical novel), *Jubal Sackett, Last of the Breed,* and *The Haunted Mesa.* His memoir, *Education of a Wandering Man,* was a leading bestseller in 1989. Audio dramatizations and adaptations of many L'Amour stories are available on cassette tapes from Bantam Audio publishing.

The recipient of many great honors and awards, in 1983 Mr. L'Amour became the first novelist ever to be awarded the Congressional Gold Medal by the United States Congress in honor of his life's work. In 1984 he was also awarded the Medal of Freedom by President Reagan.

Louis L'Amour died on June 10, 1988. His wife,

Kathy, and their two children, Beau and Angelique, carry the L'Amour tradition forward with new books written by the author during his lifetime to be published by Bantam well into the nineties.